Finding Life in the Last Season

Cover artwork by Catherine E. Doering, 2008

First published by Dog Ear Publishing
4010 W. 86th Street, Ste H
Indianapolis, IN 46268
www.dogearpublishing.net

dog ear
PUBLISHING

ISBN: 978-160844-075-7

This book is printed on acid-free paper.

This book is a work of fictional stories and personal devotions by the author. No real persons living or deceased were included in this work without permission.

Printed in the United States of America

Finding Life in the Last Season

Encouragement for the Aged
and Those Who Care for Them

by

Diane Doering

Contents

Part II Autumn: Finding Grace 41

Part III Winter: Finding Hope 79

Acknowledgments

To all of the dear people we meet in care facilities; thank you for your courage and faith.

To my family… you are amazing! Bob, you take such good care of me. You're the love of my life and my best friend. Matt and Cassie, you are awesome and I am very proud of you. Thank you for giving of yourselves to make a difference in the lives of others. I love you both.

Jesus, I love you. Thank you for the life you have blessed me with.

My heartfelt thanks to all who prayed for and contributed to this project… until the Lord thanks you Himself, *and He will*, please receive mine.

"Well done my good and faithful servant..."
Matthew 25:21

A word before…

Creating these stories and devotions over the past 10 years of ministry to the elderly has been my joy. I have met some of the most courageous and amazing individuals, and I have grown and been challenged as a result of their wisdom and strength. I have also shared in their suffering and sorrows, which as heartbreaking as that often is, has given me a greater appreciation for life and what is most important in it.

Some of these stories are lighthearted, while others deal with more painful subjects, but in them all, one thing is constant … the message of hope that is provided through the love and grace of Jesus Christ.

It is my prayer that the Lord would continue to minister through these words to those who need his encouragement, and that each of his promises would bring comfort, peace and life…especially in the last season.

Rest in His overwhelming love for you…

Diane Doering
May 2009

"And his mercy, compassion and kindness toward the miserable and afflicted, is on those who fear him with godly reverence, from generation to generation and age to age."
Luke 1:50 (The Amplified Bible)

PART I

Summer...
Finding Joy

*"Shout for joy to the Lord, all the earth,
burst into jubilant song with music."*
Psalm 98:4

This Is the Day

I don't think there is any time of year that reminds me more of the passing of time than summer. As a school-aged child, summer was the beginning of that next step into the "best part of life." Whatever age I was, the next year was the age I wanted to be. Older was always better.

I'm not sure when the "older is better" part changed. It evidently has been awhile, because I can't remember. Summer is now the reminder of how quickly time passes, and summer itself seems to be shorter each year. It comes and goes so fast that I ask, "What? That's it? Where did it go?" I don't think any season brings to mind that I am getting older each year, and that the years are moving more swiftly, than summer. But is that what God intends for me… or for you?

"This is the day the Lord has made, I will rejoice and be glad in it!" No matter how old I'm feeling or how much life I've already "used up," or how quickly the days fly by, right? It's good to stop and take a look at things from God's perspective because he places such high value on us in our old age. He is timeless and yet time is part of how he uses our lives for his purpose.

God says, *"Gray hair is a crown of splendor; it is attained by a righteous life"* (Prov. 16:31).

God says, *"Do not take advantage of a widow or an orphan. If you do they will cry out to me and I will certainly hear their cry"* (Ex. 22:22).

God says, *"I will pour out my spirit on all people. Your sons and daughters will prophesy, your young men will see visions, your old men will dream dreams"* (Acts 2:17).

God also used his people in their old age! *"Moses was a hundred and twenty years old when he died, yet his eyes were not weak, nor his strength gone"* (Deut. 34:7).

Sarah was 90 years old when she gave birth to Isaac. Wow! She said, *"God has brought me laughter and everyone who hears about this will laugh with me"* (Gen. 21:6).

It's true. You and I live in a world where a high esteem is placed on youthfulness and outward appearance. But God doesn't look at the outward appearance, he looks at the heart. He looks for the heart that seeks after him with childlike wonder, but that is seasoned with the experiences of faithful servant-hood. He sees what no one else can see… and loves us anyway! No one else can do that for us, except God, and he does it over and over again. He loves us in our weakness and in our strength. He loves us in our discouragements and in our victories. He loves us when we see the years flying by and are reminded that we are growing older… and in it he understands and offers his compassion and care for our hearts and our lives.

Yes, summer has its reminders for me, but so does the One who set the seasons in motion and remains constant in each one of them. Summer's here… bask in the warmth that comes from the God who loves you in each and every season. This is the day… so rejoice and be glad in it!

The Fruit Cellar

I've been doing a little walking of late. They say it's good for you, you know. I believe it, but that doesn't mean I am always eager to get it done. It is a good time for thinking or praying, so that's an added benefit. I'm pretty sure I talk to myself sometimes while I'm walking, and I must have done that the other day when I took a much farther route than I intended. The expression, "no pain, no gain" came to me as I was calculating how far out of my way I had traveled while my mind had been wandering. Who thought up that expression anyway? No, pain, no gain… It might be true, but it sure isn't very encouraging. When you're in pain the last thing you think about is what you're gaining! At least I don't. It's hard to be in pain, whether it be the physical or the emotional variety. Suffering, loss, grief… all of that is hard, and when we're in the midst of those times, what we might be gaining is generally the last thing on our minds. Having faith certainly helps, but pain is pain, and it still hurts.

In my grandmother's house, there was a fruit cellar. I loved it. It was the coolest place in the house on a hot summer day and it had a special smell; musty and old, but timeless. The room was spotless, like all the rooms in my grandmother's house, and every shelf was organized and lined with jars of canned fruit and vegetables… lifeless and preserved… just sitting on the shelf.

Life would be easier if we lived sitting on the shelf, just like those jars of fruits and vegetables. Preserved and disconnected from life. No longer part of the tree or the vine. No longer exposed to the elements, or tossed and tumbled by the wind. No longer needing to weather storms or endure the droughts. Life would certainly be easier and safer on the shelf… but better? No pain, no gain, remember?

Someone once said, "To love is to risk everything." It's impossible to love without being connected. It requires getting off the shelf and being involved in the lives around us. It necessitates risking hurt, loss, grief and pain. And when it seems as though it might not be worth it, it's good to remember the One who risked everything for those who would never return his love. The King of Creation who emptied himself and made himself nothing so that we would have everything. I think I'll stay connected to the Vine, and when life hurts and I'm tempted to climb back on the shelf, I'll remember the tree that He was connected to, for me, and for you. His pain, our gain.

"I am the vine; you are the branches.
If a man remains in me and I in him,
he will bear much fruit;
apart from me you can do nothing."
John 15:5

Remember

He had heard the hymn a thousand times growing up, but he thought that today was the first time he had ever listened to the words. Could that be possible? He stood in front of a group of several dozen War Veterans in a nursing home. He had accepted the invitation to be the guest speaker for their Memorial Day event, but earlier that morning regretted it, wishing he could stay home instead. Awful, he knew, but he had been so busy at work, and really wanted to spend a day with his wife and kids. It was a holiday after all.

Yet, as the aged group sang the forth verse of "A Mighty Fortress is Our God" the words echoed in his ears. *Let goods and kindred go, this mortal life also, the body they may kill, God's truth abideth still...* He knew he had sung the words before, the question was whether he believed them. In his heart, he certainly would argue that he did, but he was having a moment of truth, and the truth was that he was not eager to lose any one of those things that they just sang about. No, he was pretty sure he wanted to keep it all; his stuff, his wife and his kids. He held them in a far tighter grasp than he wanted to admit. And there he stood, in front of a room full of people who had lost some or all of those things, about to use his vast experience to enlighten them. To call it ironic was an understatement, to say the least.

He looked out again at the group that had made amazing sacrifices for homeland and freedom and suddenly knew why he was there. He was not there to speak, but to listen. Not with his ears perhaps, but most certainly with his heart. The old faces before him suddenly changed before his eyes. The years melted away as he pictured them in their youth, with their lives still ahead of them, their hopes and dreams still intact in their minds and hearts. It was a generation largely forgotten by the world; and, he confessed, by him. Moved now by compassion instead of responsibility, and awed and humbled by the opportunity that God had given him at that moment, he cleared his throat to speak.

"I came here today, on this Memorial Day, to speak to you about the importance of remembrance. On the importance of holding on to memories, no matter how painful and difficult, so that we might learn from them. But it is my day to be taught… To learn from you. Not how to hold on, but how to let go." He paused and looked around the room. Unreadable and silent faces looked back at him. He continued. "Every one of you has lived through loss. Just by your living here, in this place, you have had to let go. You have had to let go of your independence and your freedom. You have experienced the loss of family and friends, of home and of health. Many of you have lost children, and most of you your spouse. You have learned how to let go of the things that are most precious in life and yet you sit before me today with dignity and faith and I am awed by you. You have my complete respect and admiration and I am profoundly struck at this moment by what I have to learn from you. Thank you for your sacrifice, your service and your selflessness. God bless you."

He gathered his unused notes and stepped away from the podium. The applause was heartfelt and he acknowledged the group with an appreciative wave and walked out the door. He barely made it to his car before he broke down and wept. "I'm sorry," he said to the Lord, "that I did not want to come here today."

In a deeper way than ever before he understood why God commands his people to care for the widow, the poor and the orphan. He saw God reveal Himself in that room, in the faces of those who had learned to let go of the dearest things in life; people

❖

who had experienced the deepest kinds of loss and survived it. He had spoken the words so many times to himself before, "tomorrow is not promised to us, and each day is a gift," but today he had been taught what that really meant. Holding on to things tightly does not mean they can't be snatched from your grasp in an instant. Better to hold them in an open hand remembering each day how precious they are. He started his car and drove down the driveway of the facility. He was looking forward to a day with his family and knew he would appreciate it far more now. He would remember who God had used to open his eyes and heart that morning. Those who had lived, loved, lost and learned how to remember what is really important.

"As a father has compassion on his children, so the Lord has compassion on those who fear him; for he knows how we are formed, he remembers that we are dust.

As for man, his days are like grass, he flourishes like a flower of the field; the wind blows over it and it is gone, and its place remembers it no more.

But from everlasting to everlasting the Lord's love is for those who fear him, and his righteousness with their children's children..."

Psalm 103:13-17

Simplify

Simplify. A simple word, a more difficult discipline. It seems that so much of life is spent working and acquiring and trying to attain a certain status, that learning how to *simplify* almost *mystifies* us. The startling reality is that most of us will reach a point in our lives where we are forced to simplify, because we can no longer do what we once were able to. Whether we reach that point because of circumstances, illness or age it can leave us feeling somewhat "less than" our former self. Is that what motivates us to strive so hard? Are we unwilling to simplify?

Perhaps the same thoughts have run through your mind as have run through mine...

"Simplify? How could I possibly do less? I mean, someone has to do it, right?"

Or maybe this has been the hidden fear behind the excuse...

"If I don't do as much, then I might be expected to do what I am doing better, and then if I can't do it better, I'll be a failure, and if I'm a failure, no one will appreciate me, and then I won't be asked to do

anything, and then I'll be alone, and then it will be really simple, because I'll have nothing to do!"

Pretty ridiculous, but if I'm going to be honest, I would have to confess that there was a time in my life I believed that lie and others like it. And I can be fairly sure that same lie has been told to you as well. I know that, because I know that it is a trick commonly employed by the enemy of our souls to keep us too busy to spend time on what truly matters in life, all the while convincing us that our value as a person is based solely on what we can do or accomplish.

The truth is our value is not based on what we can do, but on who we are. Jesus wants us to simplify so that our value as a child of God is what motivates us to invest our time and talents in the things that make a difference in our lives and the lives of others. And He wants us to simplify so that when that day comes when we are not able to do all that once filled our days and fulfilled a purpose, we can rest in the knowledge that we are valuable to Him. If we know that we are deeply loved, completely forgiven, totally acceptable, fully pleasing and absolutely whole in Christ it's easier to simplify, because the important work has already been accomplished, by Him, for us. Those truths set us free to live simplified lives as creations of infinite worth. But just in

case you're afraid to take my word for it, let me
remind you of His:

> *"The Lord your God is with you,*
> *he is mighty to save.*
> *He will take great delight in you,*
> *he will quiet you with his love,*
> *he will rejoice over you with singing. "*
> *Zephaniah 3:17*

The Caring God

Dear Lord, I ask for help to obey You,
    And You show me a task that I don't desire to do.

I ask You to give me a heart for what You care most about,
    And You show me things that break my heart.

Jesus, you said, *"Be compassionate, even as your Father in heaven is compassionate."*

Is the only way for me to do that to allow You to do it through me?
    If I truly humble myself before You, can You use me to care as You care?

I confess to You, Lord, that it is most difficult …
    Because caring as You care, hurts.

Pain comes with caring, and You know the pain of that more than I ever could.

You know the pain of loss. You know the pain of abandonment. You know the pain of rejection.

You know the pain of being forgotten. You experienced your Father turning His back on You in the very moment You needed Him most… You were forgotten, so that I would never be.

You know what no one else knows …
    You see what no one else sees …
        You care when no one else cares.

My prayer today is that You would give me the courage,
    faith,
        obedience
           and love,

To reflect your image to those You care about, my caring
God.

And Your mercy, when I pray this prayer again tomorrow.
Amen.

"Though others may forget… I will not forget you.
See, I have engraved you on the palms
of my hands."
Isaiah 49:15

Independence Day

Sarah had lived at The Manor for two years. She considered herself fortunate. Most of the people who lived here were extremely ill or frail enough to no longer care for themselves. Sarah, on the other hand, had come to live here because her apartment in the towers had been sold to developers and all the residents of that building displaced. She was considered one of the "independent" ones. Which is why she thought it comical, as she sat with a pen and notebook in her lap, that she had been asked to write about the meaning of Independence Day for the nursing home's Fourth-of-July newsletter. Sarah had a feeling that what she had in her heart to write was not what they were looking for, and she weighed carefully her options. Deciding that she had nothing to lose she forged ahead. With crippled hands and faded eyesight, Sarah put pen to paper and shared her thoughts…

Independence Day is a celebration of our nation's freedom. It is good to celebrate that independence. I'm not against it, but I've have been thinking about the word independence itself, and it is that which I would like to share with you on this Fourth of July.

We treasure independence in our society. Perhaps because it cost so much for us to be free and independent as a nation, and even within our nation, to have freedom truly be for every person. As individuals, we place a very high importance on being independent. It is a goal at most of the crossroads of our lives to reach a new level of independence.

We raise our children to be independent. We strive in our livelihood to create enough wealth to one day be independent. We erect walls in our lives to protect our independence, greater security and privacy, all for our freedom and independence. Why, then, do we wonder when we lose our independence that we fall into despair?

To be dependent goes against everything we have been taught throughout our entire lives. We try to live life independently... alone...not asking for help or assistance. We keep ourselves as far removed from dependence on others as possible. Until one day, we need help, and we suddenly feel that we have failed. We feel as though we have become a burden. We feel as though our worth has diminished. We are no longer independent.

There are other places in the world where people do not enjoy the freedoms we have in this country. But some of those places have a deep sense of commu-

nity, of helping one another, and depending on one another throughout their lives. They still grow old and get sick, but they do not have the added heartache of feeling useless. Could we learn in our freedom to have a healthy dependence on one another? Could we learn how to need each other and be free also?

I am an old woman. I have lived a good life. I am blessed with health even in my old age. But I do miss my independence. As we celebrate our Independence Day maybe we could remind each other that it is good to need each other, too. Maybe we could reach out to someone who needs to be reminded that in their dependence they are still of great worth and are loved. That would be a very good way to celebrate our freedom. Happy Fourth of July, my friends.

Sarah put down her pen. Her fingers were aching, but her heart was beating fast. She once felt she had something to say, but it had been a while since she had been asked what she thought about much of anything. Oh, she was asked, "Are you warm enough, Miss Sarah?" or "Is that all you are going to eat on your tray?" Sometimes someone would ask her about her life growing up or about her family, but that was all that she was really ever questioned about. But today she had been asked. And she had spoken. Listening was up to someone else. Now she would rest. She would rest in the freedom that she held most dear. The freedom she had in Him.

"For the creation was subjected to frustration, not by its own choice, but by the will of the one who subjected it, in hope that the creation itself would be liberated from its bondage to decay and brought into the glorious freedom of the children of God."
Romans 8:20-21

❖

Incredible

I've been doing some research and have compiled here my findings of some of the most incredible facts about God. You may be surprised at what I've discovered.

God has huge feet. Now hear me out. I told you, I've been researching. In Isaiah 66:1 God says, *"Heaven is my throne and the earth is my footstool."* God's not boasting here. He means it. He's big.

God has insomnia. Unfortunately, it's true. In Psalm 121, it says of God, *"He who watches over you neither slumbers nor sleeps."* Isn't it comforting to know when you are having a sleepless night, you are not alone? God is watching over you.

God is an accountant. He is. Matthew 10:29 says, *"Are not two sparrows sold for a penny? Yet not one of them falls to the ground apart from the will of your Father in heaven, and even the very hairs on your head are all numbered."* Now really… who but an accountant would count hair and sparrows?

I find all of these to be amazing facts about God, but I must admit this is the one that I find most incredible:

God is irrational. You say, "I knew that, because God does things that don't make sense." And I understand that, because there are certainly things that God does that I wonder about, but that is not the incredible irrationality I'm talking about. I'm talking about what God did that was not motivated by logic, but by love: *"God demonstrated his own love for us in this: while we were yet sinners, Christ died for us."* That seems a little irrational, but wonderfully so.

Let's examine how we are molded throughout our lives in this world to think. We learn to walk, we learn to talk, to tie our shoes, to ride a bike, to read, to write, to go to college, to get a job, to be a wife, or a husband, or mother, or father, to be grandparents, to retire… then what?

Our lives are very much about striving toward that next step, until we find ourselves wondering if we have served our usefulness. And unfortunately we live in a world that does not always respect all that we have achieved just by making it through all those steps, which can make that point in our lives all the more unsettling.

But remember the irrational God who loves us. He loved us first, when we were still sinners. We did nothing to achieve or deserve that love, but he gave it freely, and gives it freely still, through his son Jesus.

Take a deep breath. You are doing what God loves best. Just being. Not doing… just being. He loves you right here, right now, at this moment. Not because of what you've done, but because you are. It seems too incredible to be true. But it is true, so receive it with joy!

God is incredibly in love with you. The earth is his footstool (but that doesn't mean he's too big to care about your needs) and his love extends further than our feeble minds can fathom. That may be the most incredible truth we can ever know. His love has no limits and there is nothing he won't do to demonstrate that love. He'll sit up all night with you… he'll keep track of every hair on your head… and he'll love you with an everlasting love. Now that's incredible!

"As the father has loved me, so I have loved you. Now remain in my love... I have told you this so that my joy may be in you and that your joy may be complete... Love each other as I have loved you... Greater love has no one than this, that he lay down his life for his friends."
John 15:9-13

The Rock

It sat on the window ledge of her room; a large, smooth, round stone. It looked something like an ostrich egg. At least that's what the girls had thought the day they discovered it while walking home from school in the third grade. They had both wanted to keep it. "I saw it first," the one friend said. A fierce discussion ensued. One girl was taller, but the other more stubborn, so home went the rock with her.

It was washed, painted with a pretty lake scene on it and proudly displayed in her room. It stayed there for years… until college. At that time, the friend wrapped it up and gave it as a "going away to school gift" to the other. And off went the rock to college. And four years later, home from college.

It was the following spring when the rock was gift-wrapped once again and given back to the first friend as a wedding gift. When the married friend moved away, the rock was given back as a "take care of the rock" gift (or something).

The rock was exchanged back and forth between the two friends for years. It might have been silly, but the rock was a symbol of a lifetime of friendship. A lifetime of tears and joys and of struggles and celebrations. Time marched on, but the rock didn't look a day older.

Today, as she looked at the rock her mind wandered back through the years. "Life. It went by so fast," she thought to herself. The rock sat unchanged on the window ledge of the room she now called home. It was one of the few possessions she had decided to bring along. She wasn't sure why. But there it was, aging gracefully. She could seldom look at it without a smile forming on her lips.

There was another Rock in her life and perhaps that is why that simple reminder on her window ledge always brought her comfort. She had found that rock much later in her life, but it was the One who sustained her now. The rock who was her Redeemer, Savior and Friend. He was the sure foundation for her times, her fortress in times of trouble. And it was Him who spoke to her now, encouraging her and breathing hope into her heart. It was His love that reminded her that while everything else may have passed way, He would never leave her or forsake her.

She whispered a quiet prayer, took a final glance at the rock on the window ledge, and closed her eyes to sleep.

"There is no one holy like the Lord;
there is no one besides you;
there is no Rock like our God. "
I Samuel 2:2

Almost Perfect

As I'm writing this, it's Monday, the twenty-fourth of July. It's my husband's birthday and it's a beautiful afternoon. There's a gentle breeze, a sunny sky, the smell of summer is in the air, and my head is full of warm memories from summers past. Perfect.

My husband took the day off from work to take our kids fishing. It's *his* birthday, and he could have done whatever he wanted, play a round of golf, go to lunch with a friend, or stay at work for that matter, but he chose this and I'm enjoying the moment.

I'm enjoying the quiet wind in the trees and the distant songbirds' serenade. Wait. Are those my children arguing over who uses what fishing pole? Yes. It is. Well, it was almost perfect.

You see, that's the thing, nothing is ever perfect. And if we go through life expecting it to be, we will constantly be disappointed. Remember what Jesus said? *"In this world there will be trouble, but rejoice, for I have overcome the world."* Jesus was telling us that life is tough, bad things happen. In this world, everything isn't perfect.

But you know as well as I do, that Jesus did not intend for us to use that as an excuse to sit back and complain. He intended for us to do what he did, constantly thanking his Father in Heaven, for *everything*.

Is there something to that? If I was continually grateful would I get tripped up less frequently by life's unexpected turns? Would the little disappointments cease to so influence my attitude? Would I be more forgiving, patient and kind? I think it's likely that would be the case.

Oh, I know, some of the things that life gives us aren't little… they're huge…sometimes they're awful and just shouldn't be. But even in those things, God is still God, and he is the one perfection we can count on. His perfect will, his perfect plan, his perfect purpose and his perfect peace. Those are real and when life's not perfect, He still is.

I look over my shoulder at the scene of my family fishing at the water's edge. I wish this moment would last forever. It won't, but it's mine for now, and my prayer is that God will remind me of it… on a day that's not so perfect.

"Every good and perfect gift is from above, coming down from the Father of heavenly lights, who does not change like the shifting shadows."
James 1:17

Nothing

Nothing. Not anything, no thing, one of no interest, value or consequence. Not at all, to no degree, something that does not exist. The absence of all magnitude, of no account, worthless.

Sounds like something we would rather not be. No one wants to be nothing. We don't want to feel that we have no value and are of no consequence. But sometimes we do, and that is a very lonely and desolate place to be. To be nothing means to have lost everything, to have nothing left, to no longer matter. To be nothing is something we work our whole lives to avoid. From our very birth we cry out to be attended to, to be fed, to be held, to be cared for. We cry out against being nothing and we never stop. We want to matter, to be something, to be someone. Not *no one*. "Please notice me, I want to matter, to have value, to be loved. Please don't leave me to be nothing." We have all cried that cry, if not in words then in actions. But sometimes the cry goes unnoticed… except by one.

There is one who hears the cry. He knows the cry. He is the cry. He made himself nothing. He knows nothing better than anyone, and yet he never fought against it, rather he chose it. He made himself nothing to be *everything* for us. And His cry is that we would know that in his eyes we could never be *nothing* but that we are someone of great value… the apple of his eye, the very crown of his creation, deeply loved and never forsaken.

When He looks at the widow, the aged, the sick and the dying, he does not see nothing. He sees every hurt, every pain, every struggle and he says *nothing* will ever separate you from me and my love for you… nothing.

When He sees the poor, the fatherless, the forgotten, the orphan, he does not see nothing. He sees the doubt, the fear, the pain of abandonment and he says, "I will give you hope and a future… to me you are everything."

When He sees the hurting, the homeless, the helpless, he does not see nothing. He sees the rejection, the despair and the brokenness, but he says, "There is *nothing* that is too hard for the Lord… I am here, for you are precious to me."

For He who made himself nothing, knows our need to be something, and feels that need to the very depth of himself. He weeps when we weep, he rejoices when we rejoice, and he feels each emotion in between. He even knows what we will not allow ourselves to feel, and has already felt those hurts on his journey to our salvation. Because He made himself... nothing.

"He had no beauty or majesty to attract us to him, nothing in his appearance that we should desire him. He was despised and rejected by men, a man of sorrows and familiar with suffering... he was despised and we esteemed him not... Surely he took up our infirmities and carried our sorrows... he was pierced for our transgressions, he was crushed for our iniquities; the punishment that brought us peace was upon him, and by his wounds we are healed."
Isaiah 53:2-5

Dear Grandmother

Dear Grandmother,

I have been thinking of you since I learned that you have not been feeling well. I'm sorry. It's been a while since I've written and I'm sorry about that, too. I know I should write you more often, but I want you to know that I think of you all the time.

The other day I was remembering our vacations at the lake. Do you remember? We used to have so much fun. Do you remember the day we went for a walk and got lost? And then we decided we would follow the shoreline to take us back and ended up falling in the lake? I remember how angry everyone was when we got home. They were worried, but we had a great time. Remember the sand dunes? Those dunes looked like they went on forever. The farther you climbed the higher they seemed to go. I have such wonderful memories of that trip. I would have never visited that place if it hadn't been for you.

I remember going to work with you at the bakery at home, too. All the sounds and the smells. And the elevator that went to the basement where they kept all the flour. It seemed like a mountain of flour. I remember the summer I worked with you there. I marveled at all of the customers that knew you by name and how you knew what they wanted before they even asked! That was amazing to me and I learned so much from you.

I remember the garden in your backyard. So many beautiful roses, the bird bath and all the wren houses. It was wonderful. There was always something cooking in the oven and I remember how you could smell it the minute you stepped on the back porch. I loved that.

I remember all of those things… maybe that's why I don't do such a good job of visiting you now that you're in the nursing home. I'm afraid to add that memory to all of the others that are so good. I know that is very selfish, but I think I've tried to keep the way things were, frozen in time because the way it is now doesn't seem right. I'm sorry because if it's hard for me, I know it's even harder for you. I suppose because I don't know what to say, or do, to make it better, I don't say or do anything, and that probably makes it worse, doesn't it?

I guess that's really why I'm writing. To let you know that I realize I have not been a very good granddaughter of late and that makes me feel really bad, especially when I think of all the things you have done for me over the years. I would like to try to do better… I hope you can forgive me. I guess I have a lot to learn. Maybe you could teach me, just like you used to.

"There is a time for everything, and a season for every activity under heaven… a time to be born and a time to die… a time to weep and a time to laugh… a time to keep and a time to give up … a time to be silent and a time to speak… He has made everything beautiful in its time."
Ecclesiastes 3:1-11

Never Late

Summer is drawing near its end. That is always a disappointment for me. I love the slower pace and warm lazy weekends. I'm not sure why the changing of the seasons makes such a difference in the way we live. I understand why it used to, when farming was a way of life for so many people, but today, living in the city, it shouldn't matter so much, and yet there is a discernable difference. I always have projects that I intend to get to over the summer months while the days are longer and I think I'll have more time. I never get to them all. My list is always too ambitious, but this year, I really fell short. And I keep forgetting to do things… does that sound familiar? It happens far more frequently than I care to admit. I've been blaming it on the lack of structure in my days, because it's summer and we have a more relaxed schedule, but I think I might be getting a little more forgetful. I forget phone messages, I forget appointments, I forget to mail things. No big deal, but I do notice that I'm doing a little more of it. And I know that is a part of growing older.

There are worse things than being forgetful… like being forgotten. Being forgotten is something that happens to all of us at one time or another. Someone forgets a birthday, or a spouse forgets an anniversary, or a "thank you" is never spoken. Each one of those may bring a little sting to our emotions, but it's when being forgotten becomes a way of life that it is most painful… and for some people that is the harsh reality. Being forgotten is a reality in our frail humanity, but not God's reality.

God sees the forgotten and remembers. He never forgets a birthday, but instead remembers the day he created each of us. There has never been a hurt feeling or a fallen tear that has gone unnoticed by Him. He has never failed to remember any important happening in our lives and he has forgiven us each time we confessed that we forgot to thank him for all that he's done. He always remembers what we need, even before we know ourselves. He loves us when we are most unlovable and he even reminds us of things we would otherwise forget. And in those times when we have prayed, and asked and cried out and God seems silent or has taken too long, he has not forgotten and he is never late… He is remembering with love the promises he has made, and kept, since the beginning of time that are available to us through his Son.

Being forgotten can be the reality of a sinful world, but being forgotten by God is something that we can be assured that we will never know… and that is very good to remember.

⸎

*"But do not forget this one thing, dear friends.
With the Lord a day is like a thousand years,
and a thousand years is like a day.
The Lord is not slow in keeping his promise..."*
2 Peter 3:8

PART II

Autumn…
Finding Grace

"The grace of our Lord was poured out
on me abundantly,
along with faith and love that are in Christ Jesus."
1 Timothy 1:14

A Season for Everything

I am sure you are familiar with theses verses but read them again with me:

There is a time for everything and a season for
every activity under heaven:
A time to be born and a time to die,
A time to plant and a time to uproot,
A time to kill and a time to heal,
A time to tear down and a time to build,
A time to weep and a time to laugh,
A time to mourn and a time to dance,
A time to scatter stones and a time to gather them,
A time to embrace and a time to refrain,
A time to search and a time to give up,
A time to keep and a time to throw away,
A time to tear and a time to mend,
A time to be silent and a time to speak,
A time to love and a time to hate,
A time for war and a time for peace.
Ecc.3:1-8

There is great deal packed into those few verses, isn't there? What is always amazing to me is how very timely they seem no matter when I read them. Perhaps the same is true for you as you read those words and say, "yes, that's the season I am in right now."

Those words from Ecclesiastes remind me of harvest time. I'm not a farmer, and no one in my family is a farmer. In fact, until I moved to Nebraska some 19 years ago, I don't think I ever gave much thought to harvest time, but I do now. I think about the picture in nature that God gives us to better understand our spiritual harvesting… the picture of planting, and watering, and nurturing, all so we have the joy of seeing things sprout and grow. But for each of those things there is a season. The seasons are different, but all a necessary part of all living things.

I recently came across a box of things that belonged to my Grandmother. She went home to be with the Lord on September 9th, 2001, just days before the terrible tragedy that would plunge our nation into a season of mourning and eventually a season of war. And as I briefly looked at the box of her belongings, I noticed the date on the newspaper I had wrapped them in… it was Veteran's Day 2001, and I remembered, as if the events had just happened, the sense of loss and pain that an entire nation was feeling at that time. I also remembered how grateful I was that my grandmother had been spared seeing that awful day in September, and the weeks and months that followed, but grateful, too, for the simple joys that I was vividly reminded that I too often take for granted.

I remembered the many times I had remarked that autumn how beautiful the fall colors were, and how the harvest time, even in our small garden, was so abundantly rich. I don't know if it was really that spectacular, or if I just appreciated it more. It was definitely a season to *embrace* all the things in life that are so precious and to *refrain* from holding on too tightly to things that don't really matter. It was a time, a season, most of us will never forget. Life goes on, however, and we move into new seasons with new challenges and new experiences. Some of them will bring us joy, some of them will bring us sorrow, but God has promised that He will be with us in each season.

I still need to go through that box of my grandmother's treasures. I'll need to decide what I should keep and what I should give up. It will be easier to do now than it would have been when I packed that box away a few years ago, but the memories attached will be bittersweet. And I know I won't be doing it alone. God has already ordained that season, and he'll be there to offer his comfort and remind me of his faithfulness. He is the same in every season and

"He has made everything beautiful in its time."

Coming Home

She sat quietly, thinking of her home and remembering the place where she grew up. She remembered the church across the street and the bells that chimed each day—once at midday and once again in the evening. She thought about the old school and the way the leaves on the big oak trees would brush against the second-story windows on blustery autumn days. She remembered the smell of the classroom, which remained the same from when she had learned there as a girl to when she had taught there as an adult. She thought about all the tidy little houses that lined the streets, with well kept lawns and gardens. She had known each family by name, or so it seemed.

There were days those memories brought her comfort, but today the loneliness closed in with the reality that she would not be going home. And even if she could, it would never be the same. Her memories had been protected by the passing years but her home had not been. Things change. The church was gone, swallowed up by neighborhood development, the oak trees cut down years ago to make room for an expanding school that now housed a community center, and the families she had known, long since grown up, moved away or passed away. No, there would not be a homecoming for her.

But before the sadness could overwhelm her, the faithful voice of her Savior spoke to her heart. He reminded her of one of his homecomings. He reminded her of the place he had spent the early years of his earthly life as the son of a carpenter… and he reminded her that when he returned to that place with his disciples, he was not welcomed and did very few miracles there because there was such a lack of faith. He reminded her that he knew the pain of not being able to return home and that he understood the pain of loneliness. He had felt those things too.

Then came the words that brought her hope… the words that kept her from giving up in the midst of heartache. The promise of her homecoming to the place prepared for her by him. The homecoming that would wipe away every disappointment forever; in a place where there would be no more hunger, or thirst, and where God himself would wipe every tear from her eyes. Yes, she would be going home, not to the sound of church bells or the smell of the classroom, but to the loving arms of her Father in heaven. With the peace that had eluded her earlier restored, she returned to her memories to rest.

"Do not let your hearts be troubled. Trust in God, trust also in me. In my Father's house are many rooms; if it were not so I would have told you. I am going there to prepare a place for you. And if I go and prepare a place for you, I will come back and take you to be with me, that you may also be where I am."
John 14:1-3

Trapped

I spoke with a couple who, in our conversation, confided that they felt alone and trapped in their circumstances, the four walls seemingly closing in around them. I encouraged them that we have all felt that way at one time or another, and while it isn't enjoyable at the time, there is usually a purpose in our struggle. And it's true, but it's also true that some will walk in circumstances that are far more painful than others. It isn't fair, as we understand fair, but it is a part of life, and most of us do encounter circumstances that have us feeling trapped.

God has a way of reminding me, though, that there is something called perspective. And he revealed a new one to me, just when I thought that I understood being "trapped."

The night I met her it was her birthday, and she was celebrating. A beautiful girl, with a wonderful sense of humor, pretty smile and infectious laugh... but trapped... trapped in a body that didn't work. Not yet thirty years old and bound to a wheelchair. She had an independent spirit and capable mind, but had never known the freedom of walking, or dancing, or feeding herself for that matter. She was trapped in dependence on others, yet from her radiated such joy. She knew Jesus, and it showed.

I had to ask myself the question, "Does that kind of joy shine through me?" I say that I know what it feels like to be trapped, but really, do I? Not in this way. It's like standing in water ankle-deep and professing to know what it feels like to drown. I cannot begin to understand that kind life, and yet in God's faithfulness he allows me to minister compassion to others, if I am willing to let him work through me. What an awesome opportunity I've been given, and yet so often ignore, or complain about. A lesson for me in humility, again.

We serve a God who understands trapped, because he was. Jesus lived life on this earth as a man. God himself, trapped in all the confines of human flesh… cold, pain, sorrow, every physical and emotional part of life he experienced to be God with us. The God who laid the foundation of the earth also slept on its cold, hard ground. He created the tree that he would be nailed to and breathed life into the human form that would disobey him, later betray him and continues to break his heart. He could erase every being from the entire face of the earth and be done with the pain, but he does not. Why? Because God is *trapped* by an unimaginable love for his creation. A love so great, that He would send his Son, so that instead of being trapped, we could be free. A love so intense that He hears all of our questions of why, when he allows what we do not understand, and cares for us in our frustrations, bitterness and disappointments. A love so pure that He doesn't hold our inability to trust him against us, but holds us close to himself instead. Trapped, by His own choosing, but trapped nonetheless. How great is the love the Father has lavished on us, that we should be called… His.

I saw her again the other day. Same beautiful smile, same sweet and gentle countenance. She told me that every night before she goes to sleep, she thanks Jesus for giving her another day. I tried to remember if I had done that the night before, then I tried to forget, because I knew the answer….

Every life will encounter difficulties, and some will bear more than others. We will all make mistakes, we will all fall short, and we will all, at one time or another feel "trapped." We are not however… we're just waiting for the freedom He gave us to become complete.

Lord, Jesus, I humble myself before you and confess that there is so very much I take for granted, and I am sorry. Please give me a heart that really understands what it means to be broken and seeks to bring healing for those who hurt. Apart from You, I have no ability to do that, but I know that through You, life, hope, comfort and peace flow freely. Thank you, Jesus, for your gift of grace that extends to me and all those who are willing to receive it. Amen.

"Though the mountains be shaken and the hills be removed,
yet my unfailing love for you will not be shaken,
nor my covenant of peace be removed,
says the Lord,
who has compassion on you."
Isaiah 54:10

Looking into His Eyes

There was an old story about a man who missed Jesus because he was looking for him in the synagogues instead of face to face. He recalled that first time he had heard it he didn't understand its meaning. He pondered that and decided he had missed the point because of a hard heart and tightly closed eyes. He was just like the man who missed Jesus, because *he* was looking in the wrong place… and he remembered that time in his life very well…

For years his career had moved him from city to city, and he never had a chance to become very connected in any place he had lived. Finally, a job became available that offered less travel and an opportunity to stay put for a while and he jumped at it. And then he jumped in. His calendar was full of bible studies, prayer groups, a men's fellowship group that did everything from play golf to camping trips, and he loved it! It was all good and it offered him something that for years he has missed. He had never felt so close to God. But then, it happened.

His mother fell ill suddenly and passed away, and his father, left alone in a farmhouse in a very remote rural area, needed help. He had a younger sister, but she had four kids and lived too far away.

He was alone, lived within a two hour drive and had more freedom, so the task fell to him. A couple of months of making that trip every weekend, and the obvious failing health of his father, made the decision for him. His dad was going to need to be moved from the family farm to an assisted living facility in the nearby town, and that was not going to be easy for anyone. The next few weeks were some of the saddest he had known, next to the passing of his mom. The life he was enjoying so much when all this happened was being put on hold.

Or was it? Was it possible that his eyes were being opened to find God outside of his religious activity? Could it be possible that he had been filling his time with *busyness* that wasn't his heavenly Father's *business*? For the very first time he asked himself if he had missed Jesus, just like the man in the story, because he was looking in the wrong place. And the answer was right in front of him.

He opened his eyes to the need of the people living in the care center with his dad. He opened his eyes to the needs of struggling families in a small town; of single mothers trying to make ends meet, of teenagers who saw a dead end by staying in a rural community, of the people who knew the end of an age was coming for the family farm. And in the eyes of each of them, he saw Jesus, and he knew he was there, for however long, to make a difference in the lives of as many people as he could. He poured himself into doing exactly that and in doing so looked directly into the eyes of his Savior and Friend. When his dad passed away fourteen months later he had no regrets, and knew that as hard as it had been, God had used his life for a much greater purpose in that time. And he knew that Jesus was as close as the next pair of eyes he looked into.

"But go and learn what this means:
I desire mercy not sacrifice."
Matthew 9:13

City on a Hill

There's a painting that hangs in the Nelson-Atkins Museum of Art in Kansas City, called *Jerusalem from the Mount of Olives*. It was painted by Frederick Church, an American artist, in 1870. It is a beautiful image of the Holy City, and the lighting is so striking it almost glows. It is easy to stand in front of that painting and get lost in it.

I hadn't thought about that painting for some time, until a warm, but overcast, September day a few years ago. On that particular day I was in a battle with what I knew I should be doing and what I wanted to do. I had felt all day that I was to make a visit to a care facility near my home, and I did not want to go. It had only been a few weeks since a dear friend of mine who lived in that facility had passed away, and I had not been back since. And, I told myself, there were so many other things that I needed to get done. But making that visit continued to invade my thoughts, as I worked away on one small unimportant project after another, I finally made my way to the car.

This particular home is only a few miles from my home, and sits high on a hill. It is a dark and rather foreboding building, built in the 1960s. On that afternoon, as I turned the corner and started making my way in that direction, I saw that building absolutely shining in the distance, illuminated by the sunshine that appeared to be bursting directly overhead though the dismal sky. I looked at that home on the hill and was instantly reminded of the painting of the Holy City… the city that Jesus wept over.

I couldn't help but wonder if He had wept over *that city* too, that city on a hill, that community of aged ones who were largely forgotten and alone. I was so sorry for my resistance all morning to hear His call and go. When I arrived, I spent a very blessed afternoon with the people there in the home on the hill. God is very patient and forgiving.

Jesus said, "A city on a hill can't be hidden." He was referring to the light that shines through all who follow him, but I know in my case for certain, that there are times I miss him by *looking* for his light instead of *being* his light. There are many cities on hills to be found. There are many places where those who are precious to God are isolated from the rest of us. They are heroes, and teachers, people we can learn from, be discipled by. And some of them are waiting for just one person to care enough to tell them that they have a God who loves them. So many forgotten ones… but not forgotten by Him.

They are not hidden from God's sight, they are in the palm of his hand, and loved with an everlasting love. And for those looking, and listening, and willing to go, God reveals himself and blesses us through them.

May God be gracious to us and bless us and make his face shine upon us, that your ways may be known on earth, your salvation among the nations."
Psalm 67:1-2

The Secret of Being Content

Have you ever had one of those moments where you are struck by the notion, "this must be what it feels like to be content;" where in that space in time you feel as though you lack nothing? It's a nice feeling, although I believe most people don't put the brakes on in their busy lives to allow themselves that experience. We're rushing to the next thing that will make us happy. True?

Webster's Dictionary defines the word *contentment* this way: "a feeling or manifesting satisfaction with one's possessions, status, or situation." Next to the definition is a date. 1526. Which means the word's earliest recorded use can be traced back that far. 1526. That's an old word, but one that probably doesn't see as much use these days.

Let's face it, we live in a world that tells us we are never to feel satisfied with our possessions, status or situation! No matter how great they are. We live in a world today that says in order to be content we need more, more, more!

Is it any wonder then when we reach a point in our lives where we have less, and less, and less, we fall into despair? The generation that is going to suffer

the most as a result of this is not my generation, the baby boomers, (although we are pretty spoiled) but the next one. It's today's kids. We have done them a horrible disservice in not teaching them about contentment. And I don't mean the dictionary definition; I'm speaking of God's definition. The Apostle Paul put it this way, *"For I have learned to be content whatever the circumstances. I know what it is to be in need and I know what it is to have plenty. I have learned the secret of being content in any and every situation, whether well fed or hungry, whether living in plenty or in want"*
Phil. 4:11-12.

Paul knew that contentment was a spiritual discipline, not just something you stumble into, but something you cultivate with practice. It was something that generations before mine were taught as they endured hard times. They were taught that contentment comes not from what you have, but from *who* you know. When God was removed from the equation on how to lead a full and rewarding life, we stopped learning that to be content with what you have is a good thing. It doesn't make a person less ambitious, or mean that they lack focus or drive. It simply means that life consists of more than status or possessions; and that you can rise above your circumstances and enjoy an abundant life, in plenty and in lack. What a concept!

I know a beautiful woman who is more than one hundred years old. She calls me "sugar" and tells my kids to "stay in school." She has been confined to a wheelchair for the last few years and lives in a nursing home where she shares a room with another woman in a space that is barely large enough to hold their two beds, two dressers and a couple of chairs. Although I've never asked, I'm guessing that's all she has left, of what she has acquired throughout her life, is in that tiny room. She is an absolute joy to be around, because she has learned the secret of being content.

She has lived a long time, and she has seen many things, both wonderful and terrible. I'm sure she has known times of great need, and perhaps there were times where she had plenty, but whatever the case may have been over the last century, she knows the secret. She has insight into that lost word and way of life and we all could learn from her.

As I write this, it is the day before Grandparent's Day. At least that's what the greeting card industry says. And it's good to honor grandparents with a note, or card, or phone call, maybe even some flowers or a gift. Any way we would choose to remember them is nice. But to really speak blessing and value into an older person's life, I think there is an even better way. Take a child and sit them on that elder's knee and ask them to teach that little one the secret of being content. It's a lesson our children will need one day… and we're running out of those who still remember how to teach it.

"Keep your lives free from the love of money
and be content with what you have, because
God has said, never will I leave you and never
will I forsake you. So we say with confidence,
The Lord is my helper; I will not be afraid.
What can man do to me?"
Hebrews 13:5-6

Have You Seen Thomas?

Thomas hadn't had much to say lately. Those who knew him best understood that he had always been this way. When he was troubled or pondering something he became very quiet. But those who didn't know him, or had never tried, mistook him for a sour old man. Of course, they couldn't be further from the truth.

Thomas was far from sour. He was simply introspective. He had grown up in a generation where quiet reflection and thinking before engaging one's mouth had been something of a virtue. He was taught that if you didn't have anything helpful to say, that it was better to keep still. Thomas was raised to believe that folks should be "slow to speak and quick to listen" and so that was what he had been doing. For a little over a month now, Thomas was just watching and listening. Thinking much, but saying little. The news had been constantly reporting the tragedy and there were many people who offered plenty to say on the matter, and of course, there were opinions on every side. But nothing from Thomas. He wasn't saying a word.

Was it that he wouldn't share his thoughts, or was it that no one asked? There was, after all, a lifetime of wisdom stored away in this quiet man. He had seen much and learned even more. There was treasure just below the surface for those who would take the time to uncover it; but just as Thomas was quiet, the questions were few and unrelated to what was happening in the outside world. No, the questions were asked of the media and the experts, not of the aged ones, who had weathered these events before. How many others like Thomas sat watching, and listening, and thinking what they might share if they were asked? What would they say?

Would they speak of God being the one with the answers instead of the television? Would they explain that horrible things happen not because God isn't caring but because mankind is flawed? Would they teach that evil is evil, and war is terrible, and death is always sad, but that God is always there? They might… if someone asked.

Have you seen Thomas lately? Or someone like him? He's been quiet, thoughtful and not had much to say… but he might, if we ask.

> *"Those who cling to worthless idols*
> *forfeit the grace that could be theirs."*
> *Jonah 2:8*

Expand My Vision

Have you ever had someone come into your life and completely change the way you looked at everything? Jesus did that with every person he came in contact with. He challenged those he encountered to see life in a new way… to see things God's way and to see things the way God sees them.

That is a very good way to pray. "Lord, please let me see the world through your eyes." When it gets tough is when God *answers* that prayer. What happens when what we see causes us to hurt? What happens when, instead of just seeing what God sees, we feel what God feels?

When we allow ourselves to do that it is amazing what is revealed and sometimes it does hurt. It hurts because this world is so far from God's created perfection. When we see what God sees, we see his children living in conflict with one another, we see division in his Body, the church, we see people living side by side but taking no interest and having no compassion on their neighbor. We see His creation hurting so badly, but numbing the pain with worthless things.

All that being said, it is still a very good way to pray. "Lord, let me see the world through your eyes." It's a good prayer, because if I see, and if I feel, then I might be moved to make a difference. I may have to start with myself, to heal the hurt within, but then I can move on… maybe I can only make a difference in one life, but maybe that life will go on to touch thousands of lives, or more! God created us to be in relationships, and he knows that it is definitely worth the pain… It cost Him *everything* to be in relationship with us.

There is life in asking God to let us see what he sees and in allowing ourselves to feel what he feels and it leads us to a deeper understanding that we were not created to do life alone. We need our Heavenly Father, and we need to be connected to one another as his children.

Have you ever had someone come in to your life and completely change the way you looked at everything? If you've met Jesus, you most certainly have… don't be afraid… just open your eyes. It might hurt, but He's promised to be right there with you, every step of the way.

*"How great is the love the Father has lavished on us,
that we should be called the children of God."*
1 John 3:1

The Door

It's amazing how the human mind works. How our memories are stored and recalled. We might recall something or someone from years ago, but forget what we intended to get out of the fridge after we've opened it. It happens to me all the time… both the forgetting and the remembering. It is quite remarkable, though, how a taste or smell, or sight or even a sound can revive a memory we thought was long gone.

When I was young we lived near an older couple and they showed a lot of kindness to me. In their living room, was a picture of Jesus. I'm sure you've seen it. It's the picture of Jesus in a garden standing at a door, knocking. I loved that picture, even though at the time I had no idea what it was about. I didn't really even have much understanding of Who it was about, but I admired it anyway.

It wasn't until years later that I would come to know Jesus, and I remember very well the first time I read the scripture from Revelation, *"behold I stand at the door and knock,"* how that image came flooding back to me. I remembered the peace and awe I used to feel whenever I looked at that picture in my neighbor's home. I understood, finally, that they had probably prayed that one day I would know what it was all about. God is merciful and patient with us.

There are those, however, that still might wonder if the door Jesus is standing before will open for them. They might be filled with peace and awe, and be drawn in as I was as a child, but then dismiss it as nothing. But it is most certainly something… It is God himself saying, "Open the door to Me." That picture depicts the invitation to open the door that Jesus stands before, and allow Him access to our hearts, and lives. If that door has remained closed for you, it's not because God hasn't wanted to open it to you, it's because he is waiting for *you* to open it.

"Behold, I stand at the door and knock;
if anyone hears my voice and opens the door,
I will come in and eat with him and he with me."
Rev. 3:20

If He's been knocking and you've been resisting, let today be the day you open the door. I know what the Lord will say when he sees you. He'll say, "Welcome home, I've been waiting for you." I can picture it now…

What's in Your Lunch?

It was a Friday afternoon, not unusual, except that it had been a week that had pretty much kept me on the run from beginning to end. I was ready for a break. My then-four-year-old daughter had just emptied her backpack onto the kitchen table to show me her work from preschool. Of all her works for the week, *and there were many*, was a coloring she was most proud of (interesting because the entire thing was colored only in red crayon), a picture of Jesus and the little boy who shared his lunch.

She told me, very accurately, the Bible story of how Jesus took five loaves of bread and two fish and fed five thousand people. She said, "The little boy shared his lunch and Jesus did a miracle." "That's amazing!" I said, looking at the drawing and wondering why if the story impacted her so, that she only used one color crayon to decorate it. (That's my issue, I know.) I asked her, "Does Jesus still do miracles?" "Yep," she said, and off she danced. I looked again at the drawing in my hand of Jesus and the little boy who had shared, and at the bottom of the page it said, *"What would be in your lunch today?"* Oh, my.

I had to ask myself, "If I shared all that I had today, Lord, would anybody get fed… or would they go hungry?" I knew the answer. That day, that week, had been no different from a long line of others. Everything I did, I tried to do my way, in my own strength, and on my own schedule. Little thought to what God might want, or how I could best serve Him, it was all about just getting it done. Sound familiar?

Do we, in our willfulness, manipulate things to fit in our little box of life? I know I do. I know even when I know I'm doing it, I do. And then, if you're like me, do you have the nerve to ask God why things are so tough? Why we are not getting the results we desire? Are we nuts? No, but He is… crazy nuts in love with us, and full of grace and wisdom. Thank you, God.

The little boy who shared his lunch. I don't think he had any expectation of being used by God. He had no plan or agenda, no schedule to keep. No weekly planner or executive assistant. No email, voicemail or text messaging. He just had *lunch*. And he gave it to Jesus and everybody got fed. What is in my lunch today? Oh, boy… little boy… little guy who shared his lunch. I could learn from you.

Dear Jesus, through all of these years, the story of the little boy who shared, so that You could multiply his humble meal, has been told. Lord, please help me see, that it's not what he offered, but that he offered all he had… and that he offered it to You. And everyone got fed.

> *"Here is a boy with five small barley loaves*
> *and two small fish,*
> *but how far will they go among so many?"*
> *John 6:9*

Left Behind

I must admit, I am nostalgic. I love exploring new places, but I love even more returning to old favorite places to re-experience smells, sights and sounds. And if that much loved place has some great history attached to it, so much the better. I know that many people share my love for old things; buildings, houses, furniture, anything with a story to tell. There are people who have dedicated their lives to preserving old things, and I'm glad.

I love to hear old stories, too, even if I've heard them before. I love to hear older people recall the happenings of their lives, their triumphs and trials, and just about the "way things used to be." I truly wish there was as much interest in preserving those treasures. Those memories are un-mined gold, buried deep in the hearts and minds of our elders. They are so willing to share them, if we'll ask.

It has become the trend, in certain places, to restore old buildings and make them fashionably "new" again. I don't mind that, I just sometimes find it ironic that such a high value is placed on those treasures, while our living treasures, our elderly are often forgotten and neglected. It makes a statement about our culture in some respects. Not a very flattering statement. It seems we show a lack of appreciation for those who can tell us so much more than an old building or piece of furniture can.

On a trip to a historic Illinois river-town, I noticed that a building partly destroyed, was left exactly as it had been at my last visit several months before. I asked about it, as this was very unusual in this afflu-ent area, and was told that the building had been rescued in the midst of being torn down by the his-torical society. Its future was being decided by the courts, whether it will be preserved or the rest of it destroyed. I thought, even at that very moment, that there are far more valuable treasures that should be lovingly cared for than a half torn down old build-ing. There are things people get so passionate about… is it misplaced priority? Sometimes.

I spend a good deal of time in care facilities for the elderly and I see living treasures every day. They are more valuable than gold and God says they are pre-cious in His sight. If they matter so much to God, shouldn't we view them as precious, too? Shouldn't we be passionate about preserving their memories and their *memory* when they pass on as being of great value? I think we should, but from what I encounter, that is not always the case in the lives of so many forgotten ones.

When Jesus talked about storing up treasures in heaven, instead of treasures on earth, I believe that was what he was talking about… placing value on what really matters. God very clearly says in his Word that we are to honor our elders, and care for the widow. Why? Because He does.

"For where your treasure is, there your heart will be also."
Matthew 6:21

The Fallen Leaf

She watched him sleeping in his favorite chair and noticed that he seemed less agitated and restless today. She was glad. It had been a very difficult week. Their doctor had said there would be times like this; that as his memory faded, and with the fewer people he recognized, the more frustrated and upset he would become. This was a part of the process, they were told.

Her husband had enjoyed a very successful career as an engineer. He was brilliant in so many ways, and loved adventure. He loved to read, travel and explore. She had always teased him that he should have a job where he could be outdoors, but he loved his work and the people he had met throughout his career. He had many friends, but they saw fewer and fewer of them. She understood why that was so, but the days for her were getting increasingly long.

She walked to the window and watched as a leaf blew across the yard and briefly stuck in a small shrub. The wind gusted again and set the leaf free, to blow down the drive and into the street, eventually out of her sight. The thought occurred to her that she envied the leaf, free to go where the wind would take it. That's how they had planned for their retired years. They had intended to travel, to be free to go where their mood might take them. They had done that for a few months, but then his health began to fail, little things at first, and then it was clear that something more was wrong.

She struggled again with the guilt that came whenever she felt sad about what had been stolen from them, from her. He was losing his life one memory at a time, but so was she. With each passing day, the man she married was becoming a stranger to her, just as she was to him. She grieved the loss, but in silence, lest anyone think her selfish.

She turned and saw that he was still sleeping soundly. She sighed and went over to the couch, turned on the lamp, and opened her book to read. Sometimes a few moments of escape in a story made the day move faster. And some days, escape would not come. She began to read, but her mind was elsewhere. The pages blurred as tears came. Today, it seemed, was going to be one of those days. She abandoned her book and wandered for a time through the house, from room to room, trying to find something else to busy her mind.

She made her way to the window and pulled back the curtain. It was getting darker. Maybe it would rain. It certainly was windy and gray... so very gray. Her mind returned to the fallen leaf, blown away by the wind, just a short while ago. The leaf whose freedom she envied.

"*I wonder*", she thought to herself, "*where it is now*"?

"*You keep track of all my sorrows…*"
Psalm 56:8 NLT

PART III

Winter...
Finding Hope

"Now faith is being sure of what we hope for and certain of what we do not see."
Hebrews 11:1

Finally Home

As she walked down the hall to Elizabeth's room she could tell that something was different. She couldn't explain it but something seemed amiss. As Sara came closer she saw that the door to Elizabeth's room was closed. It was always open.

Elizabeth kept her door open for two reasons. The first because she liked to see what was going on, but also to make sure any visitor she might have would know that she was there. She didn't get many visitors. At one hundred and three years old, she had outlived most of her family. She had grandchildren and great-grandchildren, but they lived quite a distance away and seldom were able to visit her. Her friends, long gone, even some of her younger friends who had gone to her church were not able to get around much on their own. But still, her door was always open, just in case.

Sara stood in front of the door and knocked softly. There was no answer. An aide walked by, to check on another resident. Sara stopped her and asked if she knew if Elizabeth was in her room. "I've already knocked," Sara explained, "but I know she has a hard time hearing." The aide looked at Sara briefly and then replied, "I'm sorry, but if you're looking for Elizabeth McNarry, she passed away the other night," and she walked off down the hall in the direction she had been heading before.

Sara stood in disbelief. She had just seen Elizabeth the week before. She had seemed fine. She looked at the door and noticed for the first time that the flower wreath that usually hung there was missing. No wonder it had looked so strange. Tears came, and she stood there crying softly, her hand on the doorknob of the room where her friend no longer was.

A voice from behind startled her. A small woman reached out her hand and offered a tissue. "Do you want to know about Elizabeth?" she asked. Sara nodded. "Come with me," the little woman replied. She led Sara to the sitting area down the hall and motioned to the couch near the window. When they were seated the woman began, "My name is Marie, and I was Elizabeth's best friend in this place." Sara listened as the older woman shared about Elizabeth's weariness and how ready she was to go home. She explained how her mind was sharp, but how her body was failing her more each day. Life had become very difficult for her. "No," Sara interrupted, "Elizabeth loved life!" Sara continued confused, "She never complained about anything, pain or being tired, or anything!"

Marie smiled and took Sara's hand. "Of course, she would never complain around you, dear." Marie spoke softly, "She enjoyed your visits too much, to talk about her troubles. She wanted to spend that time talking about you and your life. That's just the kind of person Elizabeth was."

Sara was beginning to realize that she had not known her friend as well as she had thought. "Can you tell me more?" she asked Marie.

"Well," Marie said, Elizabeth got some news from the doctor a couple months ago and she knew the Lord would be taking her home soon, but she didn't want anyone to know, because she didn't want that kind of attention. The only people who knew were the nurses here, and me. That's how Elizabeth wanted it."

Sara began to cry again, "I wish I would have known, I could have helped…" Marie smiled at the younger woman. "You did help, dear. You were her friend and one of her only visitors. Elizabeth thought so very much of you and was very grateful for your friendship." Now Marie's eyes filled with tears, "I was with her when she went," she said, "She just closed her eyes and went home to Him, which is exactly what she had prayed for." She stopped for a moment and dried her eyes. "Elizabeth said that the last years had been so hard. With every decline in her body she longed to go home. When her eyes failed, when her hearing worsened, when her crippled fingers wouldn't allow her to even turn the pages of her prayer book, and finally when she could no longer even dress herself… she longed to be free. To go home to see Jesus."

A while passed and the two women sat quietly, strangers just a few moments ago, now connected by a relationship lost, that had been precious to both of them. Marie spoke first, "Elizabeth said that she felt the last few weeks like she was the woman in the crowd in need of healing, but not able to come close enough to touch the hem of His garment… Well, she was finally able to reach Him, and she did." Sara was overwhelmed by the compassion and wisdom of this dear lady. "Marie," she said "I want to thank you for talking with me today. Thank you so much. I'm really glad we met." Marie reached out and took Sara's hand again, "I am too, dear," she said. "I hope you'll come and see me again… I'll leave the door open."

"Give us today our daily bread." Matthew 6:11

Who Are You?

I was watching the news and election year is in full swing. Oh boy. Approval ratings, opinion polls, every word, every action, every decision counts, and I am very thankful to not be in politics. Isn't it interesting how quickly that approval can change? It is very conditional.

It is such a wonderful thing that who we are in the eyes of others is not the way God see us! In His eyes our approval rating is based on what his Son, Jesus, did for us, not what we have done. And His approval of us remains constant, no matter if we fail, or fall, God loves us, and he does not change his opinion of us based on our words, thoughts or actions. Amazing!

I remember an interesting experience I had a few years back when I broke my foot and ended up on crutches. My approval rating went up. Well, it might not have been my *approval rating* as much as it was my *approachability rating*. It was really remarkable the gracious response I got. Doors held open, (have you noticed what a lost art that has become?) great seats in restaurants, little kindnesses due to my *impairment*. I didn't mind, it really was nice, but it was interesting that my little mishap made me…

what? I'm not sure if it brought out a more humble me (possible) or more kindness and thoughtfulness in others, but it was different. Either way, it got me to thinking about how much of how we respond to others is based on what we see, what we like, or dislike, what we are in favor of or opposed to. We are a very conditional bunch, like it or not.

Here's the good news. God doesn't operate that way. He never has, and never will. God says, "I don't look at the outward appearance, I look at the heart." Gods says, "I know when you rise, and I know when you sleep, and I know your thoughts before you say a word... and I love you anyway." God says, "Others may hurt you, or criticize you, or write you off, but I never will... I will always be there for you." Gods says, "I think you are wonderful! I think you are so great that when I think of you it makes me burst out in joyful song." God says, "If things go badly and you feel as though you are alone, don't be afraid, because I will go with you where ever you go." Who are you? You are His.

That is a very high approval rating. That approval rating never takes a dive, never dips below fifty percent, in fact, it never wavers at all. It remains perfectly constant through Gods' grace, purchased by the blood of his Son, Jesus. It's the approval rating that never changes—because the Lord never changes—and he never changes his mind, about his love for you.

> *"The Lord bless you and keep you;*
> *the Lord make his face shine upon you*
> *and be gracious to you;*
> *the Lord turn his face toward you*
> *and give you peace."*
> *Numbers 6:24-26*

Work of Art

A reporter was interviewing a 104-year-old woman and asked her what the best part about being over a century old was. "No peer pressure," she replied. Isn't that the truth! I once heard it said that old people are works of art. I couldn't agree more. Just as all babies are beautiful, with their look of angelic innocence that comes from having experienced almost nothing at all of life, older people have a quality unique to them... the beauty that comes from having experienced life, and learning to live it to the fullest along the way. A life well lived has a radiance all its own and that is certainly a work of art worth appreciating.

I remember a trip to the hospital to visit an older friend of mine that had taken a fall. I wasn't sure what I would find when I saw her, she was after all one hundred years old! When I walked into the room and saw her sitting in a chair, my first reaction was relief... my second was to recognize how extremely beautiful she was. She had such grace, and even with her tiny and frail frame, she had a presence that filled the room. When she saw me she smiled, and I was so thankful that God had crossed our paths some time before. When she passed away a few years later, I was grateful to have known her, and even more still, for all that I had learned from her. She was indeed a beautiful older person… a work of art.

I have to be honest and admit that I did not always appreciate the treasure that our older generation is. For years I was too busy, too self-absorbed to take the time to even look. It took time for me to learn to look beyond the wheelchairs and wrinkles to see the wisdom and wealth that these dear ones possess. I have learned that it is easy to miss what lies beneath if we don't slow down.

Each year as the season changes from fall to winter, and as I prepare my heart for the coming of Christmas, I make a point of remembering to take time to look. I remember the story of Jesus' birth and how Mary and Joseph looked for a place to stay but were turned away because there was no room. *Who have I turned away because I was too busy to see their need?* When the weary couple finally made their way to the manger and Jesus was born, no one but a few shepherds were there to see the Prince of Peace—the long awaited Promise. The answer to every question was born into complete obscurity and in the most humble of circumstances. *Who have I missed because I was not willing to look past the surface?*

God is indeed the master of surrounding the most amazing gifts in the most humble of wrappings. He did it in Bethlehem over two thousand years ago, and He still does it today, beckoning us to come and see. Today, I think He's asking us to take a closer look and appreciate the wonderful works of art He has created... that is each one of us.

"I praise you because I am wonderfully
and fearfully made;
your works are wonderful, I know that full well."
Psalm 139:14

The Ornament

She unwrapped them one by one and then looked at the array of ornaments on the floor around her. She had never done this alone before. Decorating for Christmas was something they had always done together. When the children had been small it had been a family activity, and then as the years passed and the kids grew up and left home, it had become just the two of them. Now, she was alone, and it was almost more than she could bear.

Everyone said the first Christmas without him would be tough. Everyone said a lot of things, at first. Right after he had passed away, there was always someone around to encourage and help, but as the months passed it became less and less, and now everyone was busy with their own lives; especially now with Christmas only a week away.

She looked around her again. *I just can't,* she thought to herself, and then one by one began the task of putting the decorations back in the box from which they had just been removed. She could remember when and where each one had been purchased, and which ones had been gifts. Some of the candles were so old the wax was discolored, but she had never been able to burn them because they all had a story to tell… until now. Now it seemed the stories had all come to an end, at least it felt as though hers had.

She kept to her work, crying softly over each returned ornament to its place in the box, until she came to one she had not remembered taking out. In fact, now that she thought about it, she hadn't seen this one for years. She just assumed one of the kids had taken it for their own Christmas tree.

She held in her hand the tiny figurine; a shabbily dressed little girl holding out a simply wrapped gift. Attached to it, was a card, with the words to a song. It was old and faded but she could still make out the print. *What can I give Him, poor as I am?* She held the tiny figure in her hands and wept. If she had ever felt poor, needy and without anything to give it was now, but as quickly as that thought came to her it was replaced by the words her husband would always say, "The most precious thing about the Lord is that what he wants most from us, is us."

She sat alone in the room that was by now growing dark and felt for the first time, in a very long time, a peace wash over her. It was not going to be an easy Christmas, but she was not alone, and she was not going to give in to despair. She was going to treasure every memory and try, with all she had within herself, to move forward. She looked down at the figure of the little girl ornament in her hands, and then brought it to her lips and kissed it. She remembered the words from Isaiah 40:11, a verse that had been her husband's favorite, *"He tends his flock like a shepherd; he gathers the lambs in his arms and carries them close to his heart."*

She closed her eyes, took a deep breath and reached into the box of ornaments. And then, she began again… this time, *unwrapping* them…one by one.

On the Way to the Manger

It happens to me every year! The holiday season has passed, Thanksgiving, and Christmas, then the New Year... What?! A new year! Has the squalor that is Christmas in America already come and gone? Are the snacks and cookies all devoured and the gifts all exchanged? Is that it?

Have you asked yourself that question, too? I have come to believe that it matters little what season of life we're in, or how busy, or not busy, we allow ourselves to become, that this happens to us. And it's at this time of year, that I have to ask myself, "Did I ever make it to the manger?"

Did I ever make it to the manger, Lord? Did I push my way through the crowds, and all of the things that were vying for my attention and my time?

Did I come to the edge of the manger and gaze and peer in to see You there? Did I allow myself the time to gaze upon Your lovely face, and let the light of Your love illuminate my world?

Did I, like Mary, store up the treasures that I witnessed in Your presence, and ponder them in my heart? Did I think about all of the promises that came true for me on the day of Your birth?

Did I celebrate that because of You, I will never be alone, because You became God with us... Emmanuel... God with me? Did I reach for Your hand and hold it, wondering at the future of that tiny palm, the one that would bear nails on my behalf?

Did I do that, Lord? And if I didn't, can I do it now? Will You help me to make it to the manger to see all that I need to see to remind me of Your love for me and for this world, that needs You so desperately? Will You pour Your living water on this thirsty ground that is my heart, and cause it to overflow with compassion, joy and peace?

Take us to the manger, Lord, and let us gaze upon Your beautiful face, and come away responding to others the way that You respond to us... with grace and love without condition. Don't let us take one more step into this New Year, Lord, before we make it to the manger.

"The Lord God says, 'The redeemed of the Lord shall return and come with singing... and everlasting joy shall be on their heads. They shall obtain joy and gladness... and sorrow and sighing shall flee away... for I am He who comforts you."
Isaiah 51:11-12

A New View

It was a New Year. He sat alone in his small room thinking about what that would mean for him. His children had visited, very briefly, over the holidays. His grandchildren were getting big. They didn't like to come and see him there, and he knew why. It was not any easy place to come to. It was harder yet to stay in.

He wheeled himself near the doorway of his room so he had a better view of the activity down the halls. They were taking down the Christmas decorations. They sure didn't waste any time; it was January 2nd. His wife used to leave the decorations up well after Christmas. "It only comes once a year, we should enjoy it," she used to say. He was glad she wasn't alive to spend the holidays in this place. It would have broken her heart. But that was how it had to be for him.

He overheard some of the staff talking. One couple got engaged, but another hired a lawyer… they were calling it quits. One family had a healthy new baby, but someone else told of a family that lost theirs. One person got a good report from their doctor, but another heard that their mother only had a few months to live. Happy people, hurting people… so many contrasting situations… all of these people working side by side each day, but going home to such different lives, all the while caring for others who were never going home again.

He wheeled himself into his room. He had once been a praying man, but he had wandered away from God. He knew it, but he just didn't know if he knew the way back. The view he had from his room wasn't much, but he thought today he might take a look anyway. It couldn't be worse than the view from the hall. He pulled back the heavy drapes that covered the window. It wasn't sunny outside, but it wasn't really dark either, just a little overcast. The trees were bare, but a patch of grass peaked through the snow, here and there. A cardinal landed on one of the tree branches and began to sing. It was muffled by the thick window glass, but he could still hear it. He closed his eyes and thought about the New Year and what it would hold. He had little hope of anything good.

A single tear rolled down his weathered face. "God, I know you're there," he prayed. "But it's been so long since I've talked to you, I don't know what to say… I guess I would say, give me a new view, because the one I have is so bleak, and I don't think I can take it." He put his face in his hands and was quiet. He felt the sun through the window glass and opened his eyes. The tree with the single cardinal perched in it, just a few moments ago, was bathed in sunlight, and was absolutely full of birds, all different kinds. Someone had hung a feeder in one of the trees and the news had traveled fast, as the assortment of songbirds took their turn at the feeder. He hadn't noticed it before, but it had vastly improved the view from his window. The view… He had prayed for a new one, and he needed it. A small smile formed on his lips. It was a start.

"You hear, oh Lord, the desire of the afflicted;
You encourage them, and you listen to their cry…"
Psalm 10:17

Cold Light

Do not be afraid, do not be discouraged... That phrase is used so many times in God's Word. And it's comforting, but difficult to explain how to *not be afraid*, or *not be discouraged*. Especially when you *are* afraid or discouraged.

This is my least favorite time of year, January. I imagine I'm not alone in that. I call it the time of "cold light." I don't know why, but the light looks different to me somehow. It's not warm like May, or even April, January's light feels cold, harsh, a little unforgiving. Oh, the feeling passes and by February, I'm over it, but in January… well, sometimes it's not so good. And what I've tried to figure out is, why? It's just a time of year. It's just a month; thirty-one days strung together with a name attached to it. So what's the big deal?

Maybe it's just what God said, *"Do not be afraid, do not be discouraged."* Oftentimes January finds me in one of those places, or both. Has that happened to you? It seems we may discover that we are either afraid of what is ahead or discouraged about where we find ourselves at the present. It is the beginning of a new year, and that results in looking both ahead and reflecting on what was behind, which can bring about both fear and discouragement… if we let it.

Oh, it's bound to happen at some point, but the encouraging part is that it brings us to the very place where God can do the very most for us; to the place where we have complete dependence on Him. There's nothing like a little fear or discouragement to help me to remember who I need to be leaning on, and trusting in. When God said don't be afraid and discouraged, He didn't mean that we would not experience those feelings, or that we shouldn't. He wanted to encourage us, that when we do… He's there. God's word is there to remind us that he is with us and that we are never alone. He's promised to love us with an everlasting love, and he's promised to never leave us, no matter what.

There's not much we can do about January. It still feels cold, harsh and a little unforgiving; but God is none of those things, and that gives us hope that whatever we've come through and wherever we're heading, we don't need to be afraid or discouraged. So bring on January.

"Have I not commanded you? Be strong
and courageous.
Do not be terrified; do not be discouraged,
for the Lord your God will be with you
wherever you go..."
Joshua 1:9

If Only

It only took her a few short days to realize the magnitude of what had happened to her life. It was the best and most beautiful long-term care facility in the area. They had toured it together a couple of years ago and really liked the place; of course *looking at*, and *living in*, were two very different things. The facility had come highly recommended, by those who had experience, and had gotten very favorable reviews in several publications. But it all came down to the sad truth… it was where you went to live when you couldn't live anywhere else.

So there she found herself, in her tastefully decorated private room; that looked just like the next room, and the next. This was now home. She would have never thought this is where she would end her days. They had planned for the possibility, but she had never allowed herself to believe that it could happen, to either one of them. She wondered if she could have prepared herself better. She was wondering about a number of things, as she had a good deal of time to wonder.

They had been very successful in life. Her husband had worked hard to build a law practice that had given her the freedom to stay at home, enjoy time with friends and do about anything else she wanted as well. They had enjoyed some very good years after his retirement, and she thought there would be many more, but he became ill quickly, and before she knew it he was gone. She had enjoyed all that had come with her husband's success, but suddenly it didn't seem all that important, especially without him to enjoy it with. They had no children; another regret. Maybe they had spent too much time building a practice, instead of taking some time to concentrate on having a family. They could have, it just always seemed it would better to wait, and then it was too late. If only they had allowed themselves the time to look for the most important things in life, instead of trying to make their lives look more important… if only.

A life lesson learned too late, she thought to herself. She wished she had someone to share her thoughts with. She wished she had someone to tell all about her "if only" thoughts. If she could, maybe she could help someone else make better choices. It would be better to have a wealth of memories of a life well lived than just wealth… in the end, all that offers is a tastefully decorated private room, that looked just like the next room, and the next.

If only. She sighed and settled back in her chair. Her husband had been the positive one, the "glass half full" one. He always said that it was important to make the best of every day, because tomorrow is not promised to anyone. She should have paid better attention. He had said other things too, but it didn't matter now, and she was tired of wondering if things could have been different. She would just sit here and wait; wait for that moment to share all of her "if onlys" with… if only there was someone to listen.

"But seek first his kingdom and righteousness,
and all these things will be given to you as well."
Matthew 6:33

New Endings

There is something magical about a first snowfall of the year and the way it transforms the landscape. The bare trees and dormant grass have a new beginning dressed in a blanket of sparkling white. It makes everything look so different, all fresh and new. Even if that first big snow comes late in the year it seems like it marks the beginning of winter; a new season.

Most of us like new beginnings. There is a feeling of anticipation and promise… it's new, and we don't know quite what to expect. As a child, that new toy brings us joy and excitement, and as we grow older we look forward to each new beginning or acquisition. The new car, the new job, the spouse, and new house, kids, dog, promotion, great vacations; and so it goes. Life really is a progression of new experiences, and on the most material level, new things. But with each new beginning there is quietly something else new creeping up on our lives… the new ending.

Everyone will have one new ending or another, but no matter what it is, none of us enjoy the time in our lives when we begin to lose more than we acquire.

The new ending is different. We lose our health, our friends or our independence. We lose our home, we lose our spouse or we lose our freedom. This marks the place in our lives where each new experience is less a beginning, than it is an ending. And with it often come grief, sadness and a loss of hope. Some of those new endings are so painful that even taking life one day at a time seems more than we can handle. But we have a promise…

We have a promise from a God who has already seen us through each new beginning and will not leave us alone in the endings. He's promised that while in this world we will have trouble, that he has overcome the world and that we have hope in every beginning and every ending because of Him. Jesus said that he *makes all things new*—both the beginnings and the endings, and he has promised that we will never experience anything without him being present and is well able to meet our every need.

The new endings that we face are never easy. Some will be more difficult than others, but God's promise to sustain us is true and faithful. With each season comes a beginning and an ending, and by His grace we are made new in each and every one.

*"I am the Alpha and the Omega,
the First and the Last,
the Beginning and the End."*
Revelation 22:13

Checkers with William

Sam couldn't remember exactly what had made him say yes. Visiting the nursing home had never been anywhere close to his thoughts before. In fact, until he was asked by a friend if he could help out, he had never even considered it. An old friend's father had been placed in a nursing home several months back, and his friend had been making the 400-mile trip every weekend, but it was getting to be too much. When his friend called to ask if Sam would be willing to visit his father every other weekend, his first response was to say that he couldn't, but he really had no reason to say no so he said he would try. "My father's name is William," his friend said, "and he likes to play checkers." And so, without really knowing why, Sam was on his way.

Sam stood at the older gentleman's door and prepared to knock, when he heard a voice from behind him. "Are you looking for someone?" He turned and saw who he instantly knew to be William. He was in a wheelchair, but was not frail and had an authority about him. "Yes, sir," Sam replied, "And I believe I've found him." William smiled and motioned for Sam to enter through the door in front of them. Sam was at first shocked by the size of the room that William shared with another man, but

William took the upper-hand and again put him at ease by joking about the fact that in a room this small he hardly ever lost the remote to the television anymore. They both laughed, and as they did, the fear and unease that Sam had felt about this visit slipped away.

And so began a friendship. Every other Saturday, he arrived a little after lunch and played checkers with William. Sam seldom won. William was a pro, and after a couple of games they would just sit and talk. At first it was about the weather, then about family. William admitted he missed his son, and was disappointed that he had taken a job out of state, but he was proud of him. They talked about football, complained about the economy and laughed at each other's jokes. They had fun together, and secretly Sam knew that William was filling a void in his life, that he had not been aware existed.

Sam had never known his grandparents, and both of his parents had died young. Being the youngest of seven children, he had never been very close to his folks. He always felt that they had expended all of their "child-rearing energy" by the time he came along, and really didn't have much time for him. Sam loved them, and had always known he was loved, but they never had much of a relationship. He had acknowledged that fact, but had never known that he missed that connection with an older person, until now. Checkers with William had become far more than a game to pass the time, or a favor for a friend. It had become something Sam looked forward to, something he enjoyed… something he was thankful for.

William made it through hip replacement surgery, and William made it through rehab, and William was back at the checkerboard after every little setback. And every other Saturday, they spent the afternoon together. Sam knew that checkers with William was not going to be forever. He saw the slow, but steady decline in William's health, and he knew that when his friend made the trip to visit every other weekend, that he saw it too. And Sam knew that William saw it, but none of them ever talked about it.

No, there were other things to talk about. For today there was the weather, and college basketball, and there was politics and the latest news headlines. And for today, there was checkers with William… and for today that was enough.

"Do not withhold good from those who deserve it when it is within your power to act."
Proverbs 3:27

Now What?

'Tis the season… for football! At our house, that season begins in August and ends in February, and we enjoy every minute of it. It's silly, but it's something we can do as a family, and as our children are getting older and the first soon to be leaving the nest, we look for activities we can all do together. And watching football is one of the favorites. I love the game itself, but I'll confess, I love the drama that surrounds the sport almost as much. And that's something that continues long after the actual season is over. Earlier in the year, I heard a coach being interviewed, and he said that at the end of the season he planned to retire. By the end of the season he had changed his mind and decided to coach another team instead. "I can't stop coaching," he said, I'm a coach. That's what I do." That happens in football. I imagine it happens in other occupations as well, but it made me stop and think… *If what we do defines who we are, what do we do when we can't do it anymore?*

We live in a society that is very influenced with titles and achievements, and that's not all bad, but if our value is based on our abilities, doesn't it depreciate immensely if we lose our ability to produce results? It shouldn't, but I'm afraid that message is delivered loud and clear in some life situations. So what do we do to correct that?

When I first made the decision to stay at home and be a "mom," I always dreaded the question, "What do you do?" I tried to come up with creative titles for my "stay-at-home mom" position, but finally I just gave up. I really did feel like my value went down as a person. *"What do I do? Well, mostly laundry, but I'm due for a promotion."* Why even try? I got over that eventually, and looking back now I thank God for every single one of those days that I was home with my kids; it is the most impacting thing I will ever do with my life, and my kids are awesome… in spite of me!

But here's the point: for a time, I did not feel valued, because what I thought defined me as a person, was something I was no longer doing, I was just being a mom instead. That's very sad, because there was a time, when being a wife and raising children was considered a very noble profession, and there was great value placed on those who did that job well. Take a look at Proverbs 31:10-11: *"A wife of noble character who can find? She is worth far more than rubies. Her husband has full confidence in her and lacks nothing of value."* Where did we get off track? There was also a time that when a person retired from their job it was reason to celebrate! What a person did for a living didn't define them as an individual; it was the means to support a family. Now it seems retirement is viewed more as being "put out to pasture." Is it possible that one of the reasons we've separated ourselves from our elders so much in our society is so that we can protect our idea of progress? I don't know... I'm just asking the question. Life goes fast, and I don't want to be asking myself in a few short years, "So, now what?"

It's a good thing we have a Father in heaven, who, in spite of all our mistakes and confusion about what is really important, loves us and places a high value on us, just because we're His. And it's a good thing to understand where our value truly lies, so that when we can no longer do what we once did, we know we still matter and are of great worth—A worth so great, Jesus gave his life, so that we might know *eternal life*, after our lives here on earth are done. *Now what?* That's what... and I for one, think that is worth living for.

> *"Are not five sparrows sold for two pennies?*
> *Yet not one of them is forgotten by God.*
> *Indeed the very hairs on your head are all numbered.*
> *Don't be afraid; you are worth more than*
> *many sparrows."*
> Luke 12:6-7

Valentine Cookies

Valentine's Day. Everywhere you look, reds, pinks, hearts and cupids! It's alright. There are holidays I like less. And after all, it's about love; and love is a good thing.

When I was growing up, my grandmother worked in a bakery. Actually she worked in a bakery for more than forty years; and as a kid, having a grandma who worked in a bakery was a very good deal. On Valentine's Day she would always bring me a box of Valentine cookies. They were shaped like hearts, bigger than my fist, with a thick layer of red and pink frosting on them. They were amazingly tasty, and I always felt really loved when I was eating one of those big heart cookies! I remember one Valentine's Day being ill; and I couldn't even *think* about eating one of those cookies. But Grandma promised to bring them anyway and had my mom put a few in the freezer for me for when I was feeling better. I remember that, I suppose, because even when I wasn't feeling very good, I still felt really loved.

That sometimes is the way it is with God. Our circumstances don't always make us feel so great, but even so, we can know we are really loved by Him.

God's love for us is constant and never changing. Even when we might be at our very lowest point, He is there loving us and ready to take us by the hand and help us back up. He's made some promises to us concerning that, and he is faithful to keep them. When God says, "I will never leave you, nor forsake you," he means it. Grandma was true to her word, but God has *never, ever* broken a promise... And He never will.

Valentine cookies are great. Even week-old, kept-in-the-freezer, Valentine's cookies are pretty good, but God's love is way better. His love is an over-whelming, always there, no matter what, all con-suming love... and that's incredible. Here's a Valentine from God to you... It comes from 1 John 4:16. It's simple, but it says it all, *"God is love."*

*"If anyone acknowledges that Jesus is the
Son of God,
God lives in him and He in us.
And so we know and rely on the love God
has for us."
1 John 4:15-16*

PART IV

Spring...
Finding Peace

*"You will keep in perfect peace him whose
mind is steadfast,
because he trusts in you."*
Isaiah 26:3

Weary in Well Doing

I continue to be amazed by what I try to do on my own strength instead of relying on the Lord's help. That lesson should have been learned long ago, but it's one I must re-teach myself almost every day. The Apostle Paul, in his letter to the Galatians wrote, *"Let us not become weary in doing good."* It must have been a lesson others needed to hear more than once, as well. Maybe there is a "weary one" reading these words today... weary of mind, weary of body, weary of spirit?

It is a discipline to learn how not to become weary. Most of us go, and go and go, until we are worn out and tense. It seems that even when we do find a small opportunity to rest, we have difficulty allowing ourselves to. The church frequently looks the same as the world in this regard. Busy is best... but is it? Could it be possible that we have forgotten how to rest?

There is a restlessness that creeps into our minds and our spirits, even when our bodies are absolutely worn out. It affects those who are caring for others, who are continually meeting needs, but whose own needs go unmet. It also affects those who are in poor health and not able to be physically active. The body is stationary, but the mind just can't slow down. That kind of weariness is most exhausting, yet rest so elusive. And as the Apostle Paul warned, there is a weariness that comes from "doing" without receiving what we need to do God's work. And what we need to receive is *rest*... the kind that God alone can provide.

Picture this with me... Jesus, in the garden at Gethsemane, a few of his disciples nodding off nearby, while all the while he, in fervent prayer, pours out his heart to his Father in heaven. It is not a picture of rest as we understand rest; the Bible says that Jesus was in anguish as he prayed. But it's an example of where to go when rest eludes us... directly to Him. No matter the circumstances, no matter the situation, no matter whether we find our bodies, minds, or souls in a state of weariness, there is only one place to receive the rest we need to continue.

God never fails to answer our cry for rest when we ask him, but it will require us handing over our burdens to him, before he answers that prayer. Whether today finds you weary in well doing, or just plain worn out, the invitation has been extended to find rest in Him.

*"Come to me all you who are weary and heavy
burdened, and I will give you rest.
Take my yoke upon you and learn from me,
for I am gentle and humble in heart,
and you will find rest for your souls.
For my yoke is easy and my burden light."
Matthew 11:28-30*

The Faded Rose

She stared back at the reflection in the mirror and sighed. What had once been the mere suggestion of creases around her eyes, were now firmly etched lines.

"They're from smiles and laughter," said a voice from behind her, "and we should wear them proudly." She turned and looked at the woman seated in the chair, still lovely in her eighty-third year. "Somehow I think you wear them better than I do, Mom," she said. "I feel like a faded rose!"

Her mother gestured toward the Bible on the nearby table and motioned for it to be brought to her. "Do you know how often God talks about flowers?" she asked. "You may feel like a faded rose, my dear, but a rose is still a rose." She looked at her mother and smiled. No wonder she has so much hope in the midst of her circumstances, she thought to herself. She has the gift of seeing others, and herself, through God's eyes. "How did you get so wise, Mom?" she teased.

Her mother's eyes slightly misted. For a moment she said nothing, no doubt remembering the hardships of raising a family alone, followed by years of struggle with a debilitating illness that had stolen her independence and worldly possessions, but had never stolen her joy. The older woman smiled softly and then answered, "We don't always receive what we hope for in life. Not everything is pleasant, and sometimes, it's just plain bad!" They both laughed.

"You must remember my dear, that what may be most difficult for us, can be used for a greater purpose. The bloom that is crushed has a sweetest fragrance, when it is cared for by the Lord. If you let Him care for you, dear, you will always have what you need, even if life doesn't give you what you want."

She opened the Bible that had been lying in her lap, and thumbed through the well worn pages. She had seen her mother do this so many times over the course of her life, looking for just the words of encouragement that she needed at the time. The older woman sighed and then read aloud from Isaiah 35, *"And the desert shall rejoice, and blossom as the rose, it shall blossom, abundantly, and rejoice, even with joy, and singing."* "My dear," she said, "You are not a faded rose in His eyes, and most certainly not in mine."

*"See! The winter is past; and the rains
are over and gone.
Flowers appear on the earth;
the season of singing has come,
the cooing of doves is heard in our land.
The fig tree forms its early fruit;
the blossoming vines spread their fragrance.
Arise my darling, my beautiful one and
come with me."
Song of Songs 2:11-13*

Off the Shelf

To say I am organized would be a bit of a stretch. I don't like clutter, so I have a "system," but it only works for me, and it only works for a while before it's just a big mess. Emotionally speaking, however, I have an organization system like no other... If it's something I don't want to deal with, I just put it away, and keep it there... for a long, long time. I know, that's not a good idea. I also know I'm not the only one, right?

I met a woman at a care facility some time ago who told me how to fix that problem I have of "emotional storage." At the time, I had no idea how profound her statement was, but since that day God has recalled it to my memory so many times. I know I will never forget it, or her.

She grew up in a small town during the depression, and of course, endured a lot of extremely hard times. The story of how she came to live at the care facility was the result of another rather tragic set of circumstances, and she explained how during that time she taught herself to paint, because it helped her to express the emotional pain that she had experienced. In her wisdom and faith, she shared that she recognized she was "stuck" emotionally, and did not want to stay there, so she worked very hard at relieving that, with the Lord's help, through learning to paint. Once she did, she loved painting so much, that she began painting for the sheer joy of it, and in doing so, even with arthritic, eighty-year-old hands, began to create beautiful works of art.

It was an inspiring story, but there was something she said that painted a mental picture for me, more impacting than her artwork. She said, "You can't keep your heartaches on the shelf. When something hurts, you have two choices, find a way to deal with the hurt and move on, or stay stuck." I thought it was a fascinating view point at the time. I wasn't as excited about it when God reminded me of it later on. *You mean my emotional storage system is flawed?*

Of course, that very wise woman was right, and the Lord was so gracious to remind me of her, in order to teach me. Emotional shelving is not the best way to deal with life's hurts. We really do only have two choices, move on or stay stuck, and shelving hurts and heartaches is the same as staying stuck. Oh, we might be moving on in other areas, but in that the place of that hurt, or anger, or bitterness, or sadness, or grief, or whatever... if we are putting it on the shelf and not asking God to bring healing and help, we are stuck. Not easy to hear, but very true.

It was one of those life lessons that I had read books about, heard sermons on and listened to teaching tapes over, and over, again, but it took a little eighty-year-old woman in a nursing home to share it to make a difference for me. God is at work in our lives all the time. Of course, it takes time to make a change. I still put the occasional trouble on the shelf, but the shelf is not as crowded as it once was, so progress is being made. And every time I attempt to emotionally store something, God reminds me of that wise woman, who painted her way through her heartaches… with His help. *"The quiet words of the wise are more to be heeded than the shouts of a ruler of fools." Ecclesiastes 9:17*

Yes, Jesus Loves Me

Little ones to Him belong, they are weak, but He is strong! You've heard it before, probably many times, because it's been around for generations. The words were published in a book in 1860, by Anna Warner. In 1862, the music was added by William Bradbury for a Sunday School teacher to use to sing to a dying young boy. It has become one of the most loved and recognizable songs in the Christian faith and has been sung by missionaries the world over to teach children about Gods' love for them.

It has had such longevity because it describes us all, young or old. *Little ones to Him belong...* of course the words were meant to describe Jesus beckoning the little ones to come to Him, but we never out-grow being God's children. And we never get tired of being reminded about God's love for us, and that he is there for us in our weakness.

Jesus said, "Don't be afraid, little flock. For your Father has been pleased to give you the kingdom" (Luke 12:32). Jesus was referring not just to little children, but to the least, the unlovable, the unre-spectable, the forgotten, the downtrodden, the despised, the rejected and the abandoned... He was referring to the "little ones" in the eyes of the world.

Those are the ones Jesus said it was Gods' great pleasure to give the kingdom to. Those are who the King of the universe says he wants to take care of. And He is well able... *we are weak, but He is strong.*

The message is the same today. Jesus invites all who are in need of him, to come. There is not one who is forgotten by Him. How do we know? *For the Bible tells us so*, over, and over again. That simple message of hope that has been sung for generations in a children's song speaks the words that every heart longs to hear... that we belong and that we matter to God.

Sing it to yourself, right now... you know the words... *Yes, Jesus loves me.*

"Beware that you do not despise a single one of these little ones.
For I tell you that in heaven their angels are always in the presence of my heavenly Father."
Matthew 18:10 (NLT)

Just Go

It had been an incredibly stressful spring, so far. While this time of year usually had Abby's spirits soaring, she was near the point of exhaustion. It was very warm and she felt like going to the park, sitting on a bench and doing absolutely nothing for the rest of the afternoon. But instead, she found herself making the journey to the "old folks" home anyway. "If Charlotte doesn't see me this week, she is going to wonder what in the world happened to me," she told herself. When Abby arrived, she parked the car in her usual spot. There was always plenty of room, she could have parked anywhere, but it was all part of the ritual, and with all of the upheaval in her life, anything stable and routine, helped her feel that she still had a small amount of control.

Abby entered the side door, and followed the long hallway that led to the stairs, avoiding the elevator. There was always activity around the elevator, and today she was not up to "small talk." She shook her head and wondered if she should have stayed home. "Great company I'll be today," she thought. Abby made her way to the second floor and then down the hall to Charlotte's room.

Charlotte's door was decorated with a picture of summer flowers that had been hanging there since last summer. "Sad, and yet, again familiar," Abby thought. A constant, in a world, that for her, was changing rapidly. She knocked and pushed the door open slightly. "Charlotte, it's me," she called. Charlotte was in her chair looking through her mail, and when she saw Abby, she smiled. "I was just looking through my mail, dear, pull up a chair." Abby sat down in one of the chairs closest to Charlotte. It had probably once been pretty, but now was faded and worn. She watched as Charlotte put the last of her mail back in its envelope and placed it on the table. The older woman looked at Abby for a moment before she spoke, weighing her words carefully. "You look tired dear," she said, "Have you not been well?" Abby was taken aback, "No Char, I'm fine… it's just been so hot, and I've been working a lot, that's all." Charlotte's face held a look of concern. "Abigail," she said, "I may be ninety years old, but I can still recognize tired when I see it… what's wrong, dear? Can I help?"

That was it. The past several months came pouring out. Abby couldn't even remember all she said, but she knew that she felt better, even though her outburst had left her a trembling mass on the floor of Charlotte's tiny room. And there she sat, while Charlotte handed her one tissue after another.

"Abby," the older woman said, "It's not good to keep things bottled up inside. We're not made for that. We are not designed to live isolated, solitary lives. That was not God's plan for us. I'm glad you came today, so we could talk."

Abby had isolated herself, but she had not realized it until that moment. She had done that to save herself from the constant uninvited advice she had been receiving all around her. The well meaning "fixers" among her friends and family had been relentless, and after a while it had been easier to pull away, but the result was that she had been left alone and afraid. Charlotte had not given her any advice and had not tried to fix her problems. She just listened.

Charlotte had learned more in her ninety years than how to recognize tiredness; she had learned the art of listening, of patience and so much more. Finally, Abby was ready to speak. "I did not come here today to unload all this on you, Char. I came to visit you… I felt badly that I had not come for so long. I told myself today, I need to *just go*… but I thought I needed to do that for you, not for me. I'm sorry." They both laughed. They had been friends for a while, but they both knew that their relationship had changed forever that day.

Abby stayed for a while longer and when she left she promised she would be back soon, and she meant it. She drove down the lane that led to the road. It looked different. It felt different. Abby had been visiting Charlotte for over a year, and had begun out of a sense of responsibility, knowing that it was a good thing, something that God wanted her to do. But today she understood it was about a relationship, a connection with another human being, a friendship with someone who had the wisdom of years. Charlotte was a friend who had experienced life, and had so much to share… and the time to share it.

Abby always prayed as she drove the lane, asking God to bless and care for all the folks there, and to care for Charlotte, but today she prayed for herself. "Thank you, Lord, for telling me to *just go*… and for meeting me today, in the person of Charlotte."

"Blessed rather are those who hear the
word of God and obey it."
Luke 11:28

Changed

Some of us don't like change. My son is the one who has the most difficulty with that in our family. He likes everything to stay the same, and with a memory like a steel trap, he makes it pretty hard to make changes without him noticing. But some change is good; and we all need it from time to time, whether we like it or not. And the truth is, if we drag our feet too long about making those changes, we might get some help.

God has a way of orchestrating change in the lives of his people. He knows we're stubborn, and he knows we like to do things our own way, but that doesn't mean he can't use us, even in the midst of the process of change. In fact, some of the most amazing heroes of the faith were used by the Lord while they were "in process." If God used them, he can use us. Really!

After all, how many times did Abraham lie and say that Sarah was his sister, instead of his wife, just because he was afraid? God still used him. He made him the father of a nation.

And David, the shepherd boy made king, who was also an adulterer and a murderer (not great hero making qualities) but later called "a man after God's own heart;" the psalms he wrote are some of the most comforting and uplifting verses in all of scripture. God changed him.

How about Peter? Big mouth, but no follow-through. That change seemed unlikely, but Jesus later said of him, "On this rock I will build my church." That's quite a transformation.

Saul, later the Apostle Paul, was a persecutor of the early church. He would have sooner killed a Christian than walk around him, but on the road he met the One he couldn't get around, and he was changed forever.

Oh the lengths God will go to reveal our need of him. The grace he extends to show us where we need to change, all the while giving us everything we need in the process. God gives us the ability to change, so that we can make a difference in our lives and in the lives of others.

Sometimes God asks us to give, and sometimes he asks us to *give in*. And sometimes he just asks us to go. It might be just one life that He wants to touch through us, one person who has a need. God asks us to go to them, and in doing that he meets two needs... theirs and ours...and then... we are changed.

*"And God is able to make all grace abound to you,
so that in all things, at all times,
having all that you need,
you will abound in every good work."
2 Corinthians 9:8*

The Story of a Father and His Son

He was the Father of an only Son… and with his son he was well pleased. He remembered so well the day of his son's birth. His beauty illuminated the dark world he was born into. It seemed only a heartbeat ago that his son took his first steps, said his first words, learned to read, learned to pray… they were very close.

His son grew into an obedient, faithful, compassionate and kind young man. Perfect really. His life was not to be an easy one. His son had tasted his share of sorrow and rejection. He had often been lonely and misunderstood. But he had never asked for special treatment. He did what his father asked and he never asked for his life to be different; until that night, in the garden. He asked his father if the cup of suffering might be taken from him. That night was long and painful for both the father and his son. It was difficult for the father to deny his child, to allow suffering, to watch his son in pain…even when they both knew it was the only way.

The father watched as his son was arrested and accused, beaten and mocked. Punished for crimes that were not his, and now the son was dying. The son was surrounded by people, some who loved him, some who hated him, and some who didn't care… but for the first time in his life, the son was alone. He was alone, because his father had left him. For that terrible moment in time, the door that had always been open, was slammed tightly shut in his face; the father on one side, the son on the other. Both of them, suffering the most intense anguish… separation from one another.

The son felt the sting of death and the weight of the sin of the world upon his shoulders, the father the pain of knowing he had allowed it to be placed there. The father turned his back and hid his face… the son cried out and gave up his spirit. It was finished… once for all.

"He was wounded and crushed for our sins. He was beaten, that we might have peace. He was whipped and we were healed… the Lord laid on Him the guilt and sins of us all…"
Isaiah 53:5-6 NLT

There are many stories of loss and suffering. There are many stories of sacrifice and pain. There are many stories of the love between a child and a parent. But there is no story that compares to the true story of *a Father that loved the world so much that he gave his only Son, so that everyone who believes in Him will not perish but have eternal life…*

Two Sisters

They were sisters, but apart from the obvious family resemblance, they could not have been more different.

One was compliant, very much the straight arrow; though a bit of a worrier, the other, a free spirit; always looking for the next adventure. Growing up, their interests had been different. One left home early, to escape her father's threats of reform school, while the other had remained behind, feeling that she was needed there.

Life led them back near each other, and now each married, they lived just a few blocks from where they had grown up. They raised their families. Circumstances sometimes brought them closer in their relationship, and sometimes it separated them. But in all times, they were sisters.

Now years passed. Their children were grown with families of their own. They both found themselves mourning the loss of their husbands and life had brought them together again. Now, the differences between them seemed more of a comfort than a conflict. What had once separated them; now drew them together. They supported, encouraged and helped one another. They even took apartments in the same building. They found themselves together almost all of the time.

Oh, they were still very different. One would lose her patience when things didn't go "just so," and the other lost everything from car keys to the jar of peanut butter; but they were there for each other. And at a time in life when they would have been alone, they weren't...They were sisters.

Some might have called it chance, but it was part of a divine plan of a loving Father. After all, what father doesn't want the best for his daughters! Especially the heavenly Father. God knows our needs before we do. He has our names engraved in the palms of his hands. He is able to care for us in every situation that comes our way, and he often provides for us in the most unlikely ways. If you don't believe me, I know of two sisters you could ask.

"You saw me before I was born.
Every day of my life was recorded in your book.
Every moment was laid out before a single
day had passed."
Psalm 139:16 NLT

In Awe Again

Spring finally arrived in Nebraska! That is a reason to celebrate! Not just that it arrived but that it is staying, not just moving immediately into summer, as is often the case. I have been enjoying these beautiful days so much. Was the winter really that long, or am I finally learning to take the time to appreciate Gods' handiwork? I hope it's the latter, because God's creation is worth the time to experience. It may have only taken the Lord six days to create our world, but he intends for us to notice and spend some time enjoying it. I really do believe that to be true.

I remember a kindergarten field trip I went on to the woods. Small children are very hungry for adventure, which means they move fast; much faster than parents of small children. They move so fast they miss a lot, but when they do slow down enough to notice something, they are in absolute awe. That is one of the most delightful characteristics of little ones… when they are in awe they don't mind letting anyone see that.

So, I'm left wondering… do we outgrow the ability to be awe-inspired by the beauty that is around us, or do we in our own adult way, move so fast we miss it? Do we need to remind ourselves to slow down, and enjoy creation? After all, God did. On the seventh day, He rested. And while He was resting, he was no doubt enjoying his creation, because, after all, it was very good. And it was good God rested, because His next creation, the crown of his creation, brought him heartache. Should we not be in awe of that? That in spite of mans fall from the perfection of God's creation, we are so loved by him?

When Jesus was going up to Jerusalem, the Bible says he saw the city and wept over it. Why? He wept because he knew all that would miss him. Jesus said, *"If you had only known on this day what would bring you peace, but now it is hidden from your eyes"* (Luke 19:41). Jesus had compassion that moved him to tears. He had awe… a Holy respect. He had compassion on his creation, on the crown of his creation…us.

I don't want to miss His peace. I don't want to miss the awe of opening my eyes each morning, and realizing that I've been blessed with another day to draw breath and be alive. How sad to miss the awe in that and to not realize until it's too late. Slowing down to admire God's creation is more than an appreciation of nature, or beauty, it is a form of worshipping the God who created us, and thanking him for each day.

Is it a more beautiful spring than we've had in years? I'm not sure, but I am in awe.

"While I live I will praise the Lord; I will sing praises to my God while I have my being."
Psalm 146:2 NKJV

Mother's Day

The window blinds were still closed, but she could see by the sunshine streaming through the slits that it was going to be a pretty day. She wondered if she was going to be able to go outside. Likely not. It was not a "full staff" day. It was usually quiet on these days and a commonly heard phrase was, "wait just one minute." In fact, Sunday was the loneliest day of the week, if one could compare. And today was Mother's Day, which meant it would seem especially so. "Well, it's just a day," she told herself. "It will be over soon." But as the morning sun peeked through the blinds, it was clear, the day had only just begun.

"I'll be there in just one minute, Miss Marnie," the nurse called in. She resented the word, "miss." She was eighty-three years old and had not been a "miss" for a very long time. She guessed she was in a difficult mood, that's what they all said about her when she talked back or corrected them. "Are you being difficult today, Miss Marnie?" they'd ask.

She thought about her name. Marnie. She didn't like the sound of it anymore. Had she ever liked it? She couldn't remember. When had the self-loathing begun? Was it always there or had it started when she couldn't take care of herself anymore? How frustrating to not be able to care for oneself. She had cared for her brothers and sisters when they were young. When you're the oldest of ten children, you learn how to take care of others and yourself!

And she had cared for her own children, too; only four of them, but still a lot of work. And she had cared for an ailing husband for three years until his death. She supposed those years had taken their toll on her health. Now here she was, confined to a room the size of a closet; four walls, a window, and a door. No wonder she was "difficult," she thought to herself.

She had sent a Mother's Day card to her daughter. She hoped it had arrived on time. You never know with the mail these days, she thought. You never know about a lot of things. She wished they would take her to breakfast so she could get back to her room. One of her children might call. It was Mother's Day, after all.

Where did the years go? This was not what she had planned. She had dreams of what her old age would be like. She would be surrounded by her family, her husband and her children and her grandchildren. Why, she had grandchildren she had never seen in person! No, this was not what she had planned.

⊹❧⊰

The nurse startled her. "Let's go down to breakfast, Miss Marnie," she said. "But first let's open up these blinds and let the sunshine in. It's Mother's Day, you know."

"Yes", she replied quietly, "I know...."

"As a mother comforts her child,
so I will comfort you...."
Isaiah 66:13

The Perfect Plan

There is a perfect balance in nature. God designed it that way. And even in the world's mismanagement of it, God's provision and complex design is revealed. He takes care of all things, from the greatest to the smallest. There is a completeness and a connectedness in God's creation; all a part of His plan; and his plan is perfect. Our plans, however, change.

Technology is a remarkable way to connect with each other. The world, they say, is smaller than ever before. With one click, we have the world at our fingertips... or do we? For all our connectedness, we seem pretty far from each other as people. And it seems we don't "complete" each other, as much as we compete with each other. Was this part of God's plan, too? Or have we wandered away again, all in the name of progress?

The world says if it's faster or stronger it's better. And while that might be alright from the material perspective, it is not true when we are talking about people. If it were true, then those who are old, or sick, or weak would not be desirable. Have we crossed the line?

Are we as connected as we think, or have we allowed progress to isolate us from each other, so that we can hide from our own need? Is it too humbling to say, "I want to be loved and appreciated?" If we do, we seem weak and needy, so we pour ourselves into work and busyness. It keeps us from recognizing the pain of our separation and gives us a false sense of security. "I am needed, not needy," we say… which is fine… until we're not.

God's plan is that we would need each other and that we would need Him. Technology can't get us there. Only God can. So where do we go to be free from the hurt of this separation and isolation? Where do we go to be connected and complete? We go to the vulnerable. We go to the weak. We go to the broken, the sick, the poor and the forgotten. We go to be needed, and we find what we need… more of Him. That's the provision. That is how we are connected and complete. That's how we are healed and helped. That is God's plan… and it's perfect.

"A father to the fatherless, a defender of widows,
is God in his holy dwelling.
God sets the lonely in families, he leads forth the
prisoners with singing..."
Psalm 68:5-6

Last Goodbye

She watched them from the doorway. They were seated side by side on the bed, their backs to her. They were looking out of the window, holding hands, not saying a word; both consumed in their own thoughts, or perhaps trying not to think at all. She couldn't be sure, but through the window beyond them, she too watched the rain falling softly.

This was the day she had been dreading for the last few weeks. Before then she had never thought about it. No one wants to have this day come, and when it does, no one is ever ready. In an hour the car would arrive that would take her mother to the nursing home; along with the two small suitcases that her mother's life had now been reduced to.

Her father would not go along with them. They were saying their goodbyes now. Oh, he would be along tomorrow or the next day, he said, but today he did not have the strength to make the trip. It was too hard. Too hard to be separated after sharing a home and a life together for all these years, and too hard to be faced with the reality of what would now be. Too hard to be reminded once again, that he could no longer care for her. Too, too hard.

She watched as her parents sat hand in hand. This tiny apartment had been their home for the last several years. It was so much smaller than the house they had raised the family in. But the house had eventually become too much for them, and in the last year, as her mother's health had failed, even the apartment presented its challenges. Finally there was no choice.

She looked around the room and noticed how out of place all of their belongings looked. She had never realized that before. Home had always been wherever her parents were. It wasn't until now, that they were being separated, that it became obvious. This was it. Nothing would be the same from this point on.

She spoke gently, so as not to startle them. "Mom... Dad... the ride will be here soon." Her father nodded but said nothing. Her mother turned to him and smiled weakly, trying to reassure him that she was fine. That was her way. That had always been her way. She was the one who put everyone else at ease. Always the peacemaker, always the one with the backup plan; now it was time to put the plan in place that everyone hopes they will never have to use. Her mother's strength had seen her through a year of illness, and her faith had kept her from giving in when the doctors had offered little hope. Now her mother would need to rely on that faith again. They both would, and it would not fail them, but it would not be easy.

The afternoon light was fading. They sat on the bed, side by side and hand in hand. They did not speak, but between them a lifetime was exchanged. And outside the window the rain softly fell.

"For He himself is our peace..."
Ephesians 2:14

❖❖❖

Conclusion

Journal Entry
Monday, September 10, 2001

I was on my way early this morning to an appoint-
ment with all of these thoughts running through my
mind. *What should I do about this? How should I
handle that? Have I made a good decision? Have I
made the right decision?* And on and on they went.

As all of these questions were racing through my
head, a field of wildflowers caught my eye. Not
only was the field full of flowers, but it was full of
geese; hundreds of them. Hovering over them was a
flock of blackbirds, and further yet above them was
a huge mass of sparrows! There were birds everywhere! That field of flowers was attracting a lot of
attention!

It was only an instant later that the Holy Spirit
recalled to my mind the verse, *"Therefore I tell you,
'don't worry' … look at the birds of the air, they do
not reap or stow away in barns, and yet your Heavenly Father cares for their needs. Are you not much
more important than they?" (Luke 6:22).*

I instantly had peace. God is all about providing for our needs, just as He cares for the birds of the air and the flowers of the field. He is even working when we don't understand; working in the spiritual realm, where we can't see with our natural eyes, but can only see with the eyes faith. Later, when my day began to unravel fast, I thought back to that moment when God had told me to quit worrying, and again, even in the midst of what seemed like disaster, He brought me comfort and eventually, peace.

Life has a way of throwing curve balls at us, and stirring up rough waters, and our emotions are subject to all of that. But if we let our emotions rule our lives, we will never have peace about anything. Jesus told us life would be this way. He said, *"In this world you will have trouble, but rejoice, for I have overcome the world."* He knows this life is but a blink of the eye, when compared to the eternity that is waiting for all who have put their hope and trust in Him. God is the one constant in this uncertain world and He never changes. His promises are always true, and His word and ways are perfect. It is because of that we can have peace in uncertain, difficult, and sorrowful times.

I am sorry that I never got to say, "I love you," to my grandmother one more time. The last time I spoke to her was the evening before she went to the nursing home. She was tired and upset, and I felt so horrible that I could not be there to help her through that painful day. It was only a week later and she was gone. But nothing could be undone, I was powerless to change what had already happened, and making the long trip to be there for her burial would not have changed anything. Even so, I wrestled with my decisions and grieved the separation.

God speaks so much about "life" in His word. Jesus said he came that we would have life in the full (John 10:10). He wants us to put our time and energy into life and living life for Him! God's focus is on life, not death, because death has already been conquered, by Him. Jesus wasn't too big on funerals. Most of them He broke up by raising the dead person back to life. Take a look at the widow of Nain (Luke 7:11), and Jairus' daughter (Mark 5:21-43) and Lazarus (John 11:1-44). Jesus waited for days to go to Lazarus, not out of a lack of compassion (for even knowing what He was about to do, He was overcome to the point of weeping) but because He wanted to strengthen the faith of His followers, and show the power of God. Still, He wept with compassion for those who were hurting, and He also wept for those who didn't understand, for those who wouldn't understand, and for those who still don't understand, that He is life.

There is always sadness with loss, and in some situations far more than others. For my grandmother, even in the sadness, it was a reason to celebrate. She was with Jesus. She had come to have a relationship with the Lord in her final year. She had understood that her salvation was in trusting Jesus Christ as her Lord and Savior. She knew she could do nothing to earn that salvation, that it was a free gift to be received… and she received it. She didn't have to wonder, or hope, or pray that she would go to heaven. She knew in her heart what God promised and she accepted that truth by faith (Romans 3:23-24, Romans 6:23, John 3:16, John 14:6, Revelation 3:20). She trusted God at His word when He said, *"If you confess with your mouth, and believe in your heart that Jesus is Lord, you will be saved "(Romans 10:9-11).*

I saw the Lord's faithfulness to keep her mostly free from pain during her last year and now she has received the ultimate and perfect healing. My grandmother was blessed with a full life. Psalm 129:6 says that one of the blessings of knowing the Lord is to see your children's children. Well, she saw her great grandchildren, and will spend eternity with them and all the other members of our family whose God is the Lord. Now that is a reason to celebrate…

The things of this world are fragile, but God is eternal, and what we do in His name has eternal value. He is Holy and His ways are higher than my understanding, but His grace and mercy are available in abundance for those who put their trust in Him. So for today, I give my life to Him as I work to communicate hope, love, and peace to those who need to hear; waiting for the day where there will be no more death, or sorrow, or crying, or pain (Rev. 21:4). While God Himself wipes every tear from our eyes…

My prayer is that you are encouraged
by the Lord's great love for you
and the life that He alone can provide
… in each and every season.

Speaking inquiries for conferences, organizations,
churches, caregiver events or radio broadcasts can
be sent to lifeinthelastseason@cox.net or
friendsoftheforgotten@cox.net

CPSIA information can be obtained
at www.ICGtesting.com
Printed in the USA
FFOW03n1714151117
43470843-42144FF